SOMETIMES THEY DIE

Detective Frank Vandegraf is familiar with acts of random violence during the committing of a crime; but the street robbery and death of a shady attorney gives him pause, as the victim seems to have been universally despised. As he struggles to make sense of a crime with not enough evidence and too many suspects, he finds he's been assigned a new partner. But before they can acclimatize to each other, the discovery of troubling new information relating to another unsolved assault and robbery will test their ability to work together.

Books by Tony Gleeson
in the Linford Mystery Library:

NIGHT MUSIC
IT'S HER FAULT
A QUESTION OF GUILT
THE OTHER FRANK
JESSICA'S DEATH

TONY GLEESON

SOMETIMES
THEY DIE

Complete and Unabridged

LINFORD
Leicester

First published in Great Britain

First Linford Edition
published 2018

A catalogue record for this book is available
from the British Library.

ISBN 978–1–4448–3600–4

Published by
F. A. Thorpe (Publishing)
Anstey, Leicestershire
Set by Words & Graphics Ltd.
Anstey, Leicestershire
Printed and bound in Great Britain by
T. J. International Ltd., Padstow, Cornwall

This book is printed on acid-free paper

1

There are those times when nothing goes right.

It always seems to happen when you're especially in a hurry. And Julie LaRoche was in an *extreme* hurry tonight. Why — *why* — did crud like this always happen to him?

His useless excuse for a secretary had left early once again — not that she was much help when she was actually there — but of course his phone never stopped ringing and he had to keep answering, and the calls were all crud. His copier jammed up just when he needed copies of a lot of documents. And of course they were all *big* documents, with a couple dozen pages each. And several times he dropped the docs and they scattered everywhere and he had to take valuable time to re-collate them. It went on and on and on. It was like a comedy of errors, and not a funny comedy.

1

The punchline to this unpleasant joke was that he was now running several hours late. He had made his third call to the escrow office asking them to stay open for him, and this time they had told him he had exactly twenty minutes to get to them before they would lock their doors and head home to families and dinners.

The elevator, of course, was taking forever, even though it was almost seven by now and the building was presumably close to empty. So he slammed open the door to the stairwell, clumsily lumbered down three flights and dashed across the building lobby to the glass double doors leading to the street. He stopped in front of his building, catching his breath in puffs and pants, looking right and left for a taxi. An hour ago there would have been a half dozen of them cruising by here. Now Institution Boulevard was nearly empty, with the barest of traffic. The sun was setting and the street was deep in shadow. While winters were mild in this city, there was a damp chill in the dark air. Julie didn't even have an overcoat with him; his only thought had been to grab his aging briefcase stuffed with his papers. He shivered slightly in his thin brown suit. When things aren't going right, they aren't going right.

He looked up and down the street. The only other person on the block was waiting inside a plexiglass enclosure at the bus stop on the corner, deep in a conversation on his cell phone. He briefly considered the bus; no, it would take too long. He had no idea when one would even come along. No cabs in sight in either direction on institution. Maybe if he got to the corner of Hunt, he'd have a better chance of flagging one down. He began to walk rapidly in that direction, jamming his briefcase under his arm to have both hands free to pull out his own cell phone and speed-dial the escrow office.

It was a long block, his feet hurt, and he was still trying to catch his breath. When the office answered the phone, he gasped out a few sentences to say he was on his way and they needed to wait for him. They *had* to wait for him — this was important! Apparently the person on the other end of the line did not find it so. Julie sputtered a few epithets and viciously stabbed his finger on the screen to end the call, so hard he almost knocked the phone out of his hand. He bobbled the phone and his briefcase and stumbled slightly before regaining his grip of both.

He almost collided with another pedestrian who had suddenly appeared and was approaching from the other direction. He started to mutter an apology and walk around the man, who took a step to the side to block him. Julie halted and looked up at him. The guy was really big and fairly young. He wore baggy jeans, a denim jacket over a gray hooded sweatshirt and a huge baseball cap pulled down over his ears. Julie hated guys like this. They wore their pants too low — hadn't any of them heard of a belt? And the way they wore baseball caps, with the brim straight and the size so big it covered their ears like a country bumpkin . . .

The guy smiled in a way Julie did not like, his eyes piercing beneath thick eyebrows.

4

'Hey, sorry, boss. Can I ask you a question? I'm kinda lost here. Do you know how I get to Hastings Street?'

'Hastings? That's like, way way over on the other side of town . . . ' Julie started waving a hand, trying to sidestep the guy and get on his way. He didn't have time to give this idiot detailed instructions to the city. What was with people? Couldn't they see when you were in a hurry and something was important? Couldn't he get a GPS, or even a map, for God's sake? The guy wasn't moving. It was like he wasn't getting the message. He seemed so *dense*.

The only other person on the block, in the bus stop enclosure, had put his phone away in his pocket. He anxiously looked up the street and at his watch repeatedly. A bus was approaching, from about a block away. Then his attention was caught by the sudden flash of motion down the otherwise empty block: two men, involved in a familiar urban pedestrian dance, stepping awkwardly one way and the other, as if to untangle themselves from one another. Suddenly they stopped, and

5

it looked as if one was handing something to the other. Then he heard two loud, sharp noises, saw one man fall to his knees, saw the other one briefly hold him up and run hands over him, then drop him. The first figure slumped to the ground as if in slow motion, first to his knees and then forward onto his face. The second took off into a fast run down the street, away from the onlooker.

The spectator to this little drama yanked his phone back out of his pocket and nervously stabbed a number onto the screen. The bus stopped at the corner and pulled away again. He remained in the enclosure, frantically speaking into his phone, all the while looking over at the fallen figure.

★ ★ ★

'Frank, how long has it been since you had a partner?'

Frank Vandegraf was standing in front of the perpetually saturated desk of his lieutenant, Hank Castillo. He always marveled at the fact that no matter how covered in paperwork the desk got, it always looked organized and tidy. There had to be six separate stacks of manila folders, looseleaf binders, and sheaves of reports in front of the lieutenant. Castillo himself was sitting back in his chair, arms folded, staring inscrutably at Frank. The two struck a contrast: Castillo dapper as usual in shirt, tie and vest, suitcoat neatly hung on his chair, graying and distinguished, the picture of corporate police work; and Frank, needing a haircut, in rumpled shirtsleeves and loose tie, hands on his hips, dutifully tolerating his summons to the office and waiting to be able to get back to his own less organized desk and his own work.

'I don't know, Lou. A while.'

'Well, I appreciate the fact you've made do without one, what with our budgetary problems around here and all. We've been trying to address that issue and slowly partner up our lone wolves as the budget allows us.'

'I'm getting along just fine. No complaints.'

The truth of the matter was, Frank was

very happy to have flown solo ever since his former partner had transferred out of Personal Crimes. It suited his temperament, and he figured it suited the temperament of many of the other detectives in his squad as well. In fact there was at least one other of his colleagues with whom he could have partnered over the past months, but to put it succinctly, the guy was a major pain. This had worked out better all around, Frank figured. He had his own way of doing things, and sometimes it was just easier to travel unencumbered. As long as he continued to clear his cases at a favorable rate, he figured, nobody would make a fuss over his being without the benefit of a partner.

Castillo nodded, a wry smile underneath his salt-and-pepper mustache. 'I've got no complaints with your performance, Detective, but this is just to let you know that we plan to address the situation in the near future and you'll be able to have a partner again soon.'

Frank was about to ask 'How soon?' but as he struggled to decide the most diplomatic way to pose that question, Castillo's desk phone rang and he grabbed it up. As he spoke tersely, he picked up a pencil that was lying right next to his free hand — the guy was so organized it was scary — and began jotting on a small notepad that was also strategically located nearby. After a moment he hung up the phone and tore the sheet off the pad, holding it across the desk to Frank.

'We'll finish this conversation later. You're up. Shooting on Institution.'

Frank hesitated a moment, not taking the paper. Castillo's eyebrows shot up.

'Is there a problem, Frank?'

'Are you sure you want to give that one to me, Lou? I've got a pile of cases . . . '

'As I said, you're up. Those cases you're running down are getting stale, if I'm not mistaken?'

Frank sighed. 'Yeah.' He was spinning his wheels on several thorny ones with no real relief in sight. Being on evening shift didn't make it easier to follow up interviews.

'Look at it this way. You'll be off evenings next week. It's always easier to pursue leads on days. Things will run smoother. And we just might have some help for you very shortly.' Castillo pointedly thrust the notepaper closer. 'You're up, Detective.'

Frank shrugged and took the paper. Castillo turned his attention back to one of the papers before him. Conversation over.

★ ★ ★

'Officer Pardo, always good to see a familiar face.'

'Detective Vandegraf, nice to see you too. Come on through.'

Frank stepped under the skein of yellow police tape that had been strung up and down the block. Already the scene was bustling with the usual personnel from the coroner's office and Scientific Investigation Division as well as several uniformed officers. Powerful arc lighting had been set up that cast a harsh glare and eerie shadows over the entire scene. Two watchful unis kept an eye on the small throng of curious onlookers gathered outside the tape. Athena Pardo, the young officer, pointed to the body lying on the concrete, partially covered with a plastic tarp, where a sad-faced man in a lab coat knelt, solemnly involved in his examination.

'The victim was apparently approached by his assailant, also male, and was shot twice at close range to the chest. He was possibly robbed before the assailant fled on foot in that direction.' Pardo pointed up the street. 'We have no witnesses as to his whereabouts after that.' Frank smiled to himself. He could always count on Pardo to be formally professional. She took herself very seriously, but, Frank had long since decided, she was a good cop: thorough, intelligent, and motivated.

She then pointed down the street in the opposite direction. 'We've got a witness who saw the shooting. His name is Cameron Wardell. He was waiting for a bus when it happened. As far as we can tell, no other witnesses.'

'Any ID on the victim?'

'Not yet. The assailant must have taken his wallet. According to the witness, he came out of one of the buildings on this side of the block. We've got two officers checking them out to see if anybody's around who might know him.'

Frank nodded. 'I'm going to talk to the ME. I'll be back.'

The medical examiner was Mickey Kendrick, which constituted a good piece of luck. Once you got by Mickey's rather morose sense of humor, he was a blessing. Behind that jowly basset-hound scowl and deadpan monotone was a sharp mind and a keen professional manner. He was thorough, straightforward and, most importantly, expeditious with results. He looked up at Frank and intoned, 'Detective Vandegraf, always a pleasure.' Mickey never *spoke*: he delivered lines as if they were dark ironies.

'Evening, Mickey. What can you tell me about our gent, here?'

'Two shots fired at close range to the chest. Probably died almost instantly. No signs of physical struggle of any kind. A mark on the back of the head where he must have fallen to the ground, postmortem for all purposes. No other marks or wounds. The shooter got close enough to him to put two bullets into him and apparently grab his wallet and run.'

'I notice he's still got his watch.' Frank pointed to the left wrist of the supine body on the pavement, the side of the body that was uncovered.

'Likely only took the time to go through his pockets. They're empty.'

'So, a straight walkup shooting, you figure.'

'Yep. Slugs are still in him. Likely small caliber. I'll be able to tell you more once I get him on a table.'

Frank looked around. 'Any idea if any shells were recovered?'

'Don't know. Possibly this was a cheap .38 revolver. Been a spate of them lately. Want to take a look?'

Mickey moved back to make room for Frank, who knelt down on one knee, pulling a pair of disposable gloves out of his pocket and snapping them on. The victim might have been in his late fifties, thinning gray hair, stocky build, in an ill-fitting brown suit more suited for springtime. Brownish blood stains had spread across the front of what had been a white shirt. It was a cold late autumn evening but the man had no coat. His eyes were wide open in a familiar death stare. Frank couldn't help but think that they still held the image of whoever had shot him — the last thing he had ever seen. His expression, though, he decided, was noncommittal; perhaps he had not had the chance to form an opinion of the attacker.

★ ★ ★

The witness stood nervously, hands in the pockets of his orange leather jacket, talking with another uniformed officer not far away. Frank pegged him for late twenties. He kept shaking his bushy blond hair out of his eyes and never stopped moving. The uni seemed to be stoically tolerating the edgy, animated chattering of the young man, nodding politely and impassively. As Frank approached, he swore he saw a flash of relief in the patrolman's eyes.

'Mr. Wardell, is that right? I'm Detective Vandegraf. I'm told you saw the incident?'

'Yeah, yeah.' Wardell nodded rapidly. He didn't seem as if he was going to stop, like one of those sports bobblehead dolls. Frank thought those things were exceedingly annoying and always had to the urge to reach out a hand and stop the head from bobbling. He had that urge at the moment with this guy. He rubbed the back of his neck and stared at the guy until he stopped. Then they just stared at each other.

Finally Frank said, 'So, can you tell me what you saw, then?'

'Oh, sure. Sorry. It really flipped me out. I mean, I've never seen anything like that . . . '

'I understand, sir. So where were you?'

He pointed up the street to the kiosk near the corner. 'I was waiting for the number ten bus there. I was looking up the street for the bus and I saw the two of them moving around up the sidewalk. There was nobody else around, so it caught my eye.'

'Moving around? How do you mean?'

'They were, like, sidestepping one another on the street. Like the one guy was trying to get around the other. They were right about there.' He pointed to the body on the ground. 'Then the one guy kind of grabbed at the other and there were a couple of loud noises, I figure shots. The one guy, further away from me, started to drop to the ground and the other guy, with his back to me, kind of leaned into him, like he was trying to grab him or something. Then the first guy was on the ground and the second guy bent over him for a few seconds, then he got up and ran off that way.'

Frank looked at the bus enclosure and estimated it was perhaps seventy feet away, maybe six or seven doors down, out of the glare of the crime-scene illumination. A bright halogen-colored light burned inside of the kiosk, illuminating it through the plexiglass windows, which seemed to accent the surrounding darkness of the street all the more. He gave a quick glance up and down the block, noting the relative remoteness of street lighting.

'About what time was this? Was it dark yet?'

'I'd say it was around seven. It was just getting dark.'

'So the light hadn't come on yet in the enclosure?'

Wardell shook his head, looking puzzled. 'I don't remember. No, I don't think it had.'

'Did you remain in the enclosure or did you approach the victim?'

'No, I stayed in there. I got on my phone and called 911. Then I just kind of shook. I guess it took me a while to shake myself out of it.'

'Did you happen to see where the victim came from?'

'No, but I'm thinking he must have come out of one of these buildings on the block. I was looking up the street now and then for the bus and I don't remember seeing anyone walking up the street.'

'You said the attacker's back was to you. Did you get a look at him at all?'

'No, not really. He was a big guy. Hooded sweatshirt. No, wait . . . he might have had a jacket over the sweatshirt. His pants might have been baggy. All I remember is his clothes were dark.'

'Was he wearing a hat or could you see his hair?'

Wardell took a deep breath and stared at the ground, trying to remember. 'I can't be sure but I think his hair was dark. I'm just not positive though.'

'And you didn't see his face, is that right?'

'No. It all happened so fast. I wasn't paying attention. I mean, you don't pay attention, you know? Just people on the street. Then something happens and you don't think to — '

'I understand, Mr. Wardell. But sometimes your mind can surprise you. Some little detail will stick out that you didn't expect. That's why I ask a lot of questions, just in case something like that pops up. Did the guy move in any way unusual?'

'Move?'

'Did he, maybe, have a limp? When he took off running, did he seem athletic, or was he kinda heavy on his feet?'

'I don't remember a limp or anything unusual. He just started running.'

'Was he fast?'

Wardell thought. 'Yes. Yes, I'd have to say he was pretty fast. He kind of took off like a deer, in fact.'

'Good. See, little things like that might be a big help to me, you never know. So he was likely fairly young then, do you think?'

Wardell nodded vigorously, his eyes lighting up. 'Yeah! Yeah, now that you mention it. He did run like a younger guy would. He moved pretty fast for a big guy.'

Frank's continuing questions of the witness didn't seem to glean any new information. He could not identify any features of the attacker. A big younger man in dark jacket and baggy pants, just maybe with dark hair. That was it. Frank gave him his card in case he remembered anything else that might be of import, and took Wardell's own contact information. He noted that the address he was given was on the other side of town from the scene of the crime.

'Just curious — are you in this neighborhood often, sir?'

'Not really. I'm taking courses so I take

the bus back and forth.'

'Courses?'

'Yeah, I'm studying internet tech. Websites and search engines and such. So I take the bus.' He shook his head and almost shuddered. 'Great luck that I happened to be here tonight, huh? I hope I never have to see something like that ever again.'

Frank nodded. There were many days he found himself wishing the same thing. He wanted to tell the guy that it never got easier no matter how many times you saw it. But all he said was, 'Okay, thank you, sir, you can go. Thanks for your help. I'll be in touch if I have any further questions.'

Wardell looked up the street. 'And there's actually another bus coming. Thanks, Detective.' He jogged off for the bus kiosk. Frank waved to the officer to let him through the taped-off area.

Frank looked up and down Institution Boulevard and pondered unhappily. There were too many cases like this: probably a crime of opportunity by a predator lying in wait on a quiet street after hours. He knew that the odds were with the perpetrator: a quick swoop and mugging, few or no witnesses, return to their own neighborhood, likely far away. Robberies like this happened regularly. They often involved pointless violence, maybe simply to gratify an attacker's brutal streak, or simply because they knew they could get away with it.

And sometimes, the victims died. Senseless deaths, the kind that especially infuriated Frank.

He had a feeling that the slugs would provide the only viable clue and that they had come from an untraceable illicit weapon. He hoped he was wrong on both counts. He turned to look for somebody from SID to consult before they left.

Officer Pardo was approaching with a distraught-looking young woman in tow, the duo looking spectral under the intense arc lights. She waved at Frank as they weaved around the techs and unis on the pavement, careful to give a wide berth to the actual body.

'Detective, this woman says she knows the victim.'

The woman nodded, eyes open wide in

alarm, lips pursed tightly. One of Frank's colleagues had once remarked on that familiar look: it was as if they had buttoned themselves up so tightly, the only place for the fear to escape was through the eyes. She looked as if she might explode at any moment.

Pardo gently put her hand on the young woman's shoulder. 'This is Detective Vandegraf. Can you please tell him what you told the officer over there?'

'Oh my God, it's Mr. LaRoche,' she stammered, running her fingers across her face.

'Do you know his full name, miss?' Frank asked.

'Julius. Julius LaRoche. He's a lawyer. His office is next to where I work.'

Now Frank had his notebook out and began to jot rapidly. 'Which building?'

She pointed to the nearest doorway, a façade with a pair of glass doors topped with a glass panel with the number 1313 painted onto it.

'We're on the third floor. He's in 312. Was. Oh my God.'

'And you're in the office next door?'

She kept nodding frantically. Now she was wiping a tear from one eye. 'Y-yes. 314. Quality Imports.'

'And . . . I'm sorry, what's your name . . . ?'

'Lucy McGinty.'

'Ms. McGinty, do you know anything about him? Is he married, does he have any next of kin, how we might get in touch with them?'

'No . . . I'm sorry. I have no idea. I just knew him to say hello in the hall.'

Frank found himself rubbing the back of his neck, a reflexive gesture when he became perplexed, which was often. He was constantly being called out on that. 'Do you think there'd be anybody still up in Mr. LaRoche's office now?'

'I . . . I don't know. He's got a partner and I think they have an assistant, but it's not a big office. It didn't look like anybody was still there.'

Frank looked at Pardo, who nodded. 'We'll go check it out.' She turned back to Lucy McGinty. 'Is there anybody else in your office who might also be able to tell us anything about Mr. LaRoche?'

She shook her head. 'No. I'm the last one there tonight.'

'Okay. Stay here with Detective Vandegraf. I'll be back in a few minutes.'

Frank watched her hustle off towards the brick building. Quite a cop, he thought. He turned back to his witness. 'I'm sorry, I know this is hard, but can you tell me anything about Mr. LaRoche that might help me understand what might have happened to him tonight?'

'I don't know. I don't know him that well. I mean, *didn't*. I would see him in the hallway to say hello. He wasn't unfriendly, exactly; he just wasn't very friendly. He always seemed in a hurry, kind of distracted.'

'What's the name of the law firm?'

'Jellicoe and LaRoche. Mr. Jellicoe is an older man. He looks like he could be in his sixties. I don't know his first name. I think it's just the two of them. I've seen different people coming in and out of there for short periods, probably clerical help. I think there's a big turnover of help for them.'

'Did you see Mr. LaRoche tonight? I

mean, earlier tonight?'

'No. We've been crunched the past couple of days with documentation and I've been working day and night. I hadn't seen him in a couple of days. He's usually out of his office. I mean, *was* . . . '

There was not much more that she could tell him and she didn't seem to show any signs of calming down soon. Frank was relieved to see Pardo returning. He hoped she could shepherd the overwrought Ms. McGinty back to her office.

Pardo was shaking her head. 'Nobody in the office. In fact I think she's the only one left on the entire floor.'

That information inspired a new wave of panic through Ms. McGinty. 'I'm the only one up there? I can't go back there! What if they came back?'

Pardo nodded reassuringly, as much to Frank as to McGinty. 'I'll accompany you back up and wait while you get your things together. Do you have a car I can escort you to?'

'Yes, thank you so much.'

Pardo smiled at Frank as they turned

to the building, an unusual departure from her usual earnestness. 'Hey, by the way, I passed the Detective's Exam a couple of weeks ago. You might not be seeing me on the street all that much longer.'

'Seriously? I'm impressed! We'll be sorry to be losing you out here, let me tell you, but some detective department is going to be very lucky.'

'Well, thank you. They'll probably stick me in Property or the like. I'm told there are going to be openings. I'll take whatever they give me.'

'I hear Personal Crimes might have an opening.'

'That would be great, but you know how that usually works. There's a waiting list for your unit. They'll promote someone with time from another department.'

'No doubt breaking down doors to get to work with me. Well, good luck, Officer.'

Pardo guided a shaking McGinty back through the throng once again.

That got him thinking again: he really hoped he wasn't going to get saddled with a partner soon. Maybe he was getting too set in his ways. The joke around the unit was that he was a dinosaur. Pardo was right: Personal Crimes seldom got newbies. The unit was a preference for many detectives from other units. The chances were better that someone with experience would get transferred in. Maybe even someone as old as Frank. A new dinosaur.

Dinosaurs, he reflected, didn't tend to get along well together. Too set in their individual ways. On the other hand, it would be easier than having to break in a green newcomer. Either way, it seemed like a lose-lose.

He was yanked from his unhappy reverie by one of the SID techs in a bright blue jumpsuit. 'Detective, are you done with the body? Okay if we finish up processing?'

'Sure. Doesn't look like there's much to process. Were there any shells?'

'Negative on that. Probably shot with a revolver.'

'Any other detritus anywhere around the body?'

'Nope. We've printed his clothes but frankly, there's likely not going to be anything. His pockets are empty. There are no defensive wounds, probably no chance of skin or hair from the assailant.'

'Go for it,' Frank said, waving a hand. 'With my blessing.'

There was nothing else he could do here tonight. He headed back to the unit to see if he could find a contact number for Julius LaRoche. Perhaps there was a wife or even a family. He hated having to do it this way, late at night, but there was no alternative. In general he didn't like the evening shift, and this was one reason why. Frank was at heart a leg man. He felt most comfortable running down leads and contacts in person. That was generally difficult after eleven o'clock at night.

Sitting at his desk computer, he found two phone listings in the city for a Julius LaRoche. One was the Institution Avenue office of Jellicoe and LaRoche, attorneys at law. The other seemed to be a residential land line, something that was quickly becoming an endangered species.

He looked at his watch: almost midnight. He took a breath and dialed the number. No answer. Not even voice mail. After a dozen rings he hung up. He'd have to return in the morning to talk to LaRoche's partner and anyone else in the building he could find.

His shift was over shortly. There was nothing else he could do right now. He walked over to the watch commander sergeant and informed him that he was clocking out and would be returning in the morning.

'You really love this job, don't you, Frank?' the sergeant said wryly.

2

'Julie's dead? Are you kidding?' Carl Jellicoe was a tall, lean man with a prominent beak of a nose. He looked to be in his sixties, and not an easy sixties at that. He sat back behind his desk, regarding Frank with shining dark eyes peering out from under bushy white eyebrows, his mouth curled in a scowl. 'The hell you say!'

'Yes, sir. A robbery outside the building last night.'

'So you just told me,' Jellicoe said dismissively. Frank stood before the desk looking down at the man, thinking that he reminded him of a character out of a Charles Dickens book he read in school. There were just the two of them in the room this morning.

'So you don't mind if I sit down and ask you some questions about Mr. LaRoche?' Frank reached for a chair without waiting for a reply. He already had his notebook in hand. Jellicoe impatiently waved him into the seat.

'I've got a dozen years on Julie, but I somehow always knew I'd outlive him.'

'And why is that, sir?'

'Because Julie LaRoche is a schmuck, and always has been.'

'Excuse me?'

'I presume you know the word, Detective . . . is it Vandecamp?'

'Vandegraf, sir. I'm just surprised to hear you say that. You and he were partners, were you not?'

'For eighteen years, yes. And I'm not sure we could stand each other for most of that time.'

'That's highly unusual, wouldn't you say?'

'We stayed out of each other's way. To be honest, I don't know if either one of us could have found anyone else to get along with any better. Kind of like a marriage of convenience.'

'Speaking of marriages: is Mr. LaRoche married — I mean, was he? Is there a Mrs. LaRoche?'

'Divorced. Twice. Long ago. The exes

31

might be around somewhere, who knows. He never spoke of them and I doubt he had any dealings with them. Julie was immensely more palatable viewed from a long distance.'

'Family? Kids? Anyone?'

'One daughter from the first marriage. No idea where she might be. You might call her estranged.'

'Close friends?'

'Clearly you didn't know him.'

'Not the warm and fuzzy type, I take it.'

The old man managed an enigmatic smile. 'I was probably his best friend and I hardly knew him. Probably didn't even like him, at that.'

'And yet you worked together for almost twenty years?'

'Have you ever heard the concept of parallel play, Detective? We worked together pretty well because we knew to leave each other alone most of the time. He had his arena and I had mine.'

Frank looked around the cramped office, filled with old file cabinets and heavy, distinctly unfashionable wooden furniture. 'What kind of law do you practice here, exactly?'

'When we started out we did a lot of personal injury but now it's mostly property law. Julie was more concerned with his own property holdings than in any clientele in recent years. I don't think he's had an actual client in a couple years now.'

'Property holdings?'

'Julie liked to acquire property. He'd flip buildings, redevelop. He must have sold a few dozen buildings around the city. That's pretty much how he spent his time nowadays, buying and selling. It was like a giant board game, but with real money. Anything requiring *law*, like representation or, the almighty forbid, actually going to court, generally fell to me.'

'How's business been?'

'Abysmal. But on the bright side, it's getting worse every day. I'd retire, but how can I give up living the dream?'

Good thing, thought Frank, he hadn't tried his hand at stand-up comedy. 'Just curious, Mr. Jellicoe, why do you say you thought you'd outlive Mr. LaRoche?'

'To be honest, I thought someone might show up and kill the SOB.'

'Someone did, sir.'

'Yes, but from what you tell me, it was a random act of violence, a holdup gone bad, right?'

'So it would seem.'

'I always figured someone would walk in the door with a gun or knife or a flamethrower and just take him out. I honestly was a little concerned I might be collateral damage.'

'You're saying he had enemies, then?'

'If he knew 'em, he hosed 'em, Detective.'

'Nice guy, sounds like.' It couldn't hurt to explore this a little bit, he decided. 'Anybody he was specifically making unhappy at the moment?'

'Let's see. He recently won a negligence settlement against a charitable religious order when he was injured on their property. For *that*, he would have walked inside a courtroom, had it been necessary, which it ultimately wasn't. Then there was the apartment house he converted to condos and evicted twenty-seven fixed-income tenants.'

Frank paused, pencil in hand, mouth agape.

'And of course there's the pending purchase of the Bodega Building.'

'Bodega Building?'

'That's what he's been calling it. It's a three-story building in a neighborhood that's becoming gentrified. He wanted to gut it and turn it into commercial space. There are only a few tenants upstairs, but it presently houses a couple of mom-and-pop stores on the ground floor. There's a Cuban grocery and some kind of Central American restaurant that are well established in the neighborhood. So he called it the Bodega Building. He was going to give them walking papers the moment the deed was in his hand, which would have been any time now. He seemed to have had some confrontations with at least one individual recently.'

'Where is this building?'

'Over on San Mateo near Parker.'

'Would you say these disagreements were pretty strong?'

Jellicoe shrugged. 'I had nothing to do with any of Julie's goings-on. In fact I made a point to avoid them whenever possible. I just heard about them, or over-heard snippets if they happened to spill over to my office now and then.' This, Frank asked himself, was the man's *partner*? 'What's the difference? You just said he was killed in a robbery.'

'Sometimes things aren't the way they look, Mr. Jellicoe. Everything is always worth looking into, just in case.'

'Yes, well, he's been complaining about the intransigence of certain tenants. He said he was laying the groundwork to just throw them out the moment he owned the building. I swear he sneered in glee at the prospect.'

Now Frank really was feeling like he had fallen into a Charles Dickens novel. Julius LaRoche, it would seem, was a true piece of work. He sighed. 'Did Mr. LaRoche have any redeeming characteristics, as long as we're on the topic?'

Jellicoe snorted a laugh. 'Well, his mother was many years departed, but I'm sure when she was alive, he was totally beastly to her.'

'If I could get his home address, that

would be a help.'

'Certainly. Why not? Not like you're going to invade his privacy now.' Jellicoe recited an address which Frank jotted down: the same as that attached to the personal phone number he had tried last night.

'You have clerical staff here?'

'We've got a girl. She's fairly new. Recent college grad, I think. Works part time, mostly filing and taking calls but also doing our administrative work. We've got a recurring staff turnover here. Not only is the pay terrible, but the working conditions are execrable.' He snorted again. 'I suppose they'll get somewhat better now, though. I can't imagine I'm the easiest person to work for, but compared to Julie, I'm the offspring of Dale Carnegie and Saint Francis of Assisi.'

'Did she do any of the work on any of Mr. LaRoche's activities?'

'It would make sense. If she did any work at all, which is dubious.'

'When will she be in, or where can I reach her?'

Jellicoe looked at his watch. 'Should

have been here by now.' His desk phone suddenly buzzed. He picked it up, looking aggravated. 'Yes? I mean, Jellicoe and La . . . oh, who is this . . . ? Why aren't you here, Ms. Tarkenton? Well, hurry up then. No, thank you, I don't want anything.' He slammed the received down. 'She's standing in line at the coffee joint downstairs. What time is it?' He pointedly looked at his wristwatch. 'I'd complain about the quality of our help but it's the best we can actually get.'

Frank rose from his seat. 'I'm going to go down and intercept her to talk to her. Do you mind if I keep her from you for a few more minutes?'

'Why not? The office is going to hell in a handbasket anyway. Having to deal with Julie's detritus is just going to be the frosting on the cake around here.' He waved his hands around. 'Even in death, Julie's going to be a pain in the neck.'

'She's in the coffee shop across the street? What's Ms. Tarkenton look like?'

'Dark hair, glasses, nondescript.'

That should be a big help. He dropped one of his cards on the desk. 'Please contact me if you have anything else that might be of help. I might be back, Mr. Jellicoe. Thanks for your time.'

'I'll count the minutes, Detective.'

Frank paused at the door. 'I was just wondering. Are you familiar with Dickens?'

'Dickens. You mean Charles Dickens, the writer?'

'Uh-huh.'

'*Christmas Carol, Oliver Twist?* Vaguely. When I was younger, I always liked the actor Alistair Sim as Scrooge. Why?'

'No reason. Just asking.'

★ ★ ★

'This is terrible news. Poor Mr. LaRoche. He was mugged? Right outside our building?'

Carl Jellicoe had described Marielle Tarkenton reasonably well after all. Frank might be a seasoned detective, but he would have been challenged to describe her beyond her dark hair and glasses. She was about as average-looking a person as he had seen: average height and weight, average voice, average eye color (it looked gray but he couldn't quite be sure). What she was, however, was nervous. She nervously gulped her coffee, nervously babbled, and nervously twitched at the table where they sat in the coffee bar while people bustled back and forth past them. A painfully self-conscious twenty-something, he decided to himself. It wasn't the ideal place to talk, but he preferred to catch her outside of the office. This would have to do.

'I'm afraid so. I'm hoping you can help me out in finding the person who did this.'

'Of course, of course, but . . . how can I help? What could I possibly know?'

'I'm hoping you can tell me something about Mr. LaRoche himself: who he associated with recently, what he was working on, if there was anybody he might have particularly alienated, that type of thing. And if you know anybody I could talk to who knew him well.'

'Wow!' she exclaimed, eyes widening. 'You think it wasn't a robbery then? You think someone disliked him enough to . . .?'

'Just looking at everything possible, Ms.

Tarkenton. Maybe there's some connection that will help me find the killer.'

'Wow!' she said again. 'This is like a TV show! I don't know of any friends or family Mr. LaRoche had. He never had any personal visitors, you know?'

'There must be contact information for him at the office. Emergency contact, that sort of thing.'

'No, that's the funny thing. I don't think he had anything like that on record.'

'I understand he was involved in some transactions lately that were kind of hostile? A liability suit, some tenant evictions?'

'Well, yes. I've only been working there about three weeks, you understand. I couldn't tell you about anything before that. But recently, things like that, yes.'

'Tell me about the lawsuit.'

'Julius LaRoche versus the Little Sisters of Mercy Home for Women and Children. He stumbled on their pavement and in reaching to steady himself, slashed open his hand on a rusted metal bannister in front of the stoop of their building.'

Frank just kept liking this guy more and more. 'What was the outcome?'

'The insurance company settled with Mr. LaRoche. They usually do, in my understanding.'

'For how much?'

Tarkenton hesitated for a moment. '$75,000. Oh, I guess I wasn't really supposed to divulge that, it was confidential. Well . . . him being deceased and you investigating his murder and all . . . '

Her fussing was getting on his nerves. 'Seventy-five? Seriously?'

She nodded.

'Were there possibly any outspoken critics, shall we say, of this whole thing?'

'There was a small editorial in the paper about it, I remember. Very critical. Apparently Mr. LaRoche had a reputation for what they called 'nuisance lawsuits.' They referred to him as 'litigation happy.''

'You mean the *Blade-Courier*.' It was the city's last remaining regular paper.

'Yes, that's right.'

Great, thought Frank. The guy's sterling character had been public knowledge. There could be a list of people who had it in for him that could fill a small telephone book. 'How long ago was this settlement?'

'About two weeks. It was one of the first things he gave me to work on.'

'I'll probably need to look at the background on that case.'

'As long as it's okay with Mr. Jellicoe.'

'It will be, I'll make sure of that. And the eviction cases?'

'You must mean the condo conversions at Webleyview. That was before I arrived, but I've done a lot of the paperwork. Some of the prior tenants have been contentious.'

'So the process has been less than friendly?'

She stared at him blankly. 'They're evictions. I guess those usually aren't happy occasions.'

'Okay, but were any of the individuals particularly unhappy? Were there legal challenges, maybe personal exchanges with Mr. LaRoche?'

'Legal challenges, yes. A local attorney filed on behalf of several of the tenants.'

'So the conversion is still in legal limbo?'

'Yes. It's generated a lot of paper, let me tell you.'

'And personal exchanges? Did anybody,

say, come to the office to confront Mr. LaRoche?'

'Just the reporter.'

Frank stopped short and resisted the urge to plant his palm on his face. 'Reporter?'

'Yeah. She works for some tabloid give-away. One of her relatives was an evictee. She came up to interview Mr. LaRoche. He had no interest in it and they got kind of loud yelling at each other.'

'What was this reporter's name, do you remember?'

Tarkenton bit her lip and rolled her eyes skyward. 'I don't recall. You could look up her article that she wrote last week.'

How much better was this going to get? 'Which paper?'

'I'm not sure. One of those free tabloids that come out on Thursday.'

'Your office doesn't keep a file on published articles and editorials relating to your cases?'

She raised her hands as if experiencing a revelation. 'Oh, of course. I think Mr. LaRoche was considering suing her. I have a file of the clippings back at the office.'

'Speaking of which, I don't want to get you in trouble with Mr. Jellicoe for taking so long, so let me just ask you a couple more questions and let you get back to work. Tell me about the Bodega Building.'

'That's the building he was about to buy on San Mateo. What about it?'

'His plan was to evict the shops that are currently there, was it not?'

'Yes. I heard him one day talking to a prospective architect for the project. It was going to be mixed use, condos on the top floor, high-end office suites below, and shops and an expensive restaurant on the ground floor.'

'In that neighborhood? That's kind of a working-class area.'

'It's gentrifying rapidly. Mr. LaRoche was betting on the trends in the next few years.'

Frank sighed. Was this guy for real? 'He hadn't completed the sale yet?'

'It was supposed to go into escrow this week. In fact when I left yesterday, he was on the phone with the escrow office to try to get papers signed that day. He was impatient to get everything underway.'

45

'What time was that?'

'Around two. I had to leave early. Dentist appointment. He had me call them a couple times earlier but as I was leaving, he was back on the phone with them again.'

Employer and employee of the year, thought Frank to himself. 'Any particular reason for his impatience?'

'I think he was trying to pre-empt a legal challenge of some sort by one of the tenants. The way he put it yesterday morning was that he was going to cut their legs out from under them.'

'Out from under who, exactly?'

'The Del Oso family. They operate the grocery store in the building.'

'And were there any words between the Del Oso family and Mr. LaRoche?'

'Mr. Del Oso came to the office one day with another younger man. They had a polite but awkward conversation.'

'You were present for it?'

'Not exactly. I was asked to bring in some files while they were talking, and I saw Mr. Del Oso when he left. As I said, the interaction was polite, no raised voices or anything. But the atmosphere was very chilly. He's a kind of intimidating person, quiet but very intense.'

'Could you locate any of the documents pertaining to the purchase?'

'They must be in the office, unless Mr. LaRoche had taken them. I would think he was trying to get to the escrow office last night before they closed.'

'He didn't have a briefcase with him when he was found. Let's take a chance on the office.' Frank closed his notebook and pushed his chair back. 'I'll accompany you back and talk to Mr. Jellicoe about getting access to those files.'

Jellicoe had not truly counted the minutes before Frank's return and seemed not all that happy to see him return with Tarkenton, but he grudgingly agreed to allow access to LaRoche's office and records. Frank could have gotten a warrant for everything and that would have meant returning for still another time, a contingency Jellicoe did not seem to find all that palatable. He seemed mostly upset that Ms. Tarkenton's time would be devoted to helping Frank for the next half hour.

LaRoche's office was even more darkly oppressive than Jellicoe's, but it was reasonably tidy. Tarkenton quickly located the records he requested, as well as the file of newspaper clippings, and dutifully made copies for him, but could not locate any paperwork on the expected Bodega Building escrow. She found earlier correspondence on the pending purchase but nothing from the past week.

'Is it possible he had the papers with him when he was — you know?' she asked Frank.

'If so, the assailant took them. He had nothing, certainly not a briefcase or a file of any kind. Even his pockets were empty.'

'Well, they don't seem to be here. He had them on his desk yesterday.'

'The escrow company he was dealing with — do you know their name?'

'Yes. It was Rovendale. I remember typing up the papers.' She gave him an address.

Frank perused a few more files and finally decided he had everything he needed for the moment. Tarkenton assembled the copies in a manila envelope and handed it to him. 'Thank you, Ms. Tarkenton, I appreciate your help.'

'I hope you find whoever did this to Mr. LaRoche. What a terrible thing.'

'One last question. Did he have a cell phone?'

'Yes, he did. He used it constantly. When he wasn't on the office line he was on his cell.'

'So he would have had it with him when he left here last night, you'd think.'

'I should think so.'

Frank thanked her again and on his way out stuck his head into Jellicoe's office to say thanks and apologize for taking up his time. Jellicoe nodded silently, not even looking up from a file, clearly only wanting to see the last of Frank Vandegraf.

'If I need anything further, I'll give you a call,' Frank said.

'If you really have to,' Jellicoe murmured.

★ ★ ★

He decided to drive to LaRoche's home. The address was in Sunnyview, the northernmost district of the city. The neighborhood was pleasant, upscale, suburban. LaRoche's house was hardly opulent, but comfortable, the front yard well-tended but with just a bit of seediness creeping in at the edges, as if the gardener or the landscaper hadn't come by in recent weeks. Frank noted a car in the driveway: LaRoche's? If so, he apparently didn't drive to work. Nobody answered the bell, and it looked dark and empty through the windows. Nobody answered the door of the neighbor to the left. When he rang the doorbell of the neighbor to the right, a tired-looking woman of about forty answered and looked at him quizzically until he identified himself.

'Mr. LaRoche? Has something happened to him? I hardly know him. We've been neighbors for years, but he keeps to himself. Probably exchanged a dozen words over the years. One time he yelled at my kids for chasing a ball onto his front lawn.'

Sounded like the right guy. 'How long has he lived here?'

'I'd say he moved in here, oh, fifteen years ago. Had a wife at the time. She hasn't been around in many years now.'

'Did you ever talk to her, or do you remember anything about her?'

'She was very nice. Her name was Violet, or something like that. Something floral. Rose, maybe.'

'Any idea where she might have gone to?'

'Or Lily. It might have been Lily. No, we never got very close, but she was always much more cordial than her husband. She would smile and say hello. He would just nod and grunt at us. Always seemed to be in a hurry.'

'Any kids?'

'When they first moved in, there was a teenager who would come to visit. She stopped coming. I have no idea who she was.'

'And the wife . . . '

'Or it might have been Daisy.'

' . . . about when did the wife leave the house?'

'Oh, it had to have been ten years ago now.'

'So it's just been Mr. LaRoche since then?'

'As far as I know.'

'I need to find his next of kin, or somebody to notify. Do you have any idea where I could look?'

'I'm sorry, Officer . . . '

'Detective, actually.'

'Detective, I mean. I don't think anyone in this neighborhood could help you. I think he pretty much kept to himself, do you know? I never saw him socialize.'

Another thought occurred to him. 'Does he have a gardener or someone who comes by to tend the property?'

'There's a guy that comes and mows and blows. I don't know who he is. He doesn't come all that often anymore, maybe every three or four weeks. Usually on a Tuesday morning if I remember right.'

The remainder of the conversation was equally productive. Frank thanked her and departed, giving the deserted avenue a look up and down before getting in his car. Nothing promising here. The station was more or less on his way home so he decided to stop off there, drop off his pile of copies, maybe make another call or two, then return for his shift that evening. It would be nice to return to day shift next week.

★ ★ ★

It was already a busy Thursday morning on the unit: detectives and officers scurrying about and talking loudly, everybody multitasking to try to catch up on crazy workloads. The city was always generously dropping something new on the detectives' doorstep, and it was always a challenge to stay on top of it all. He loved the oddness of the name of his unit, Personal Crimes. Some years back it had been called Special Crimes and before that Robbery-Homicide, but at some point a commission had decided Personal Crimes had a more meaningful ring to it, the sound of a true mission statement. They still dealt with basically the same types of felony offenses: murders, severe assaults, serious robberies. The unit that handled burglaries and similar non-violent crimes had been re-named Property Crimes, which to his thinking was somewhat more lackluster. Frank had to wonder who would ever want to transfer to something called Property Crimes. It was probably where Athena Pardo was going to wind up. Frank dumped the manila envelope on his desk and plopped into his chair, taking a deep breath as he switched on his computer.

Once he would have pulled out a hefty telephone book and thumbed through it to find a number. Now even a Neanderthal like himself used his computer to look up a contact. He found Rovendale Escrow and picked up his desk phone to call. When a very harried-sounding man answered, Frank identified himself and said he was inquiring about Julius LaRoche.

'So what ever happened to that guy, anyway?' the escrow man replied with a deep tone of impatience. 'He bugged me over and over yesterday to push through a bunch of papers, then he bugged me to stay open late, and then he never showed up, and he's not answering his phone this morning! Now there's a cop calling me about him? What'd he do, shoot some-body?'

There seemed to be something about Julie LaRoche that just brought out the best in people. 'Actually, sir, somebody shot *him*. He's dead.'

'Are you kidding me? When? What happened?'

'He seems to have been killed on his way over to your office last night.'

'Good lord! Tell me it had nothing to do with the protests over the building!'

'Protests over the building?'

'Yeah. The Bodega Building. The one he was buying. He was trying to ram through the sale, make it a done deal. That's why he kept prodding us night and day that we weren't moving the paper-work fast enough to his liking. This doesn't have to do with that, does it?'

'At this point it appears to have been a robbery gone bad, Mr . . . ?'

'Roven. Ross Roven. Because that would be absolutely horrible publicity. So it had nothing to do with the Bodega Building?'

'The property on San Mateo he was

trying to buy, you mean?'

'That's the one. That's not the real name of the building. I don't know that it's got a name. It's just what he called it, so we started calling it that. Not everyone there was happy about it.'

'At the moment, most likely not, Mr. Roven. But we're looking into everything. I want to talk to you some more about this, but first of all I need to know if you can refer me to anyone who knew Mr. LaRoche. And then I'd like to know if you have copies of the documents he was supposed to sign last night?'

'Someone who knew him, no. Documents, sure. Had them all prepared and waiting for him. Too bad about what happened. So somebody just came up and shot him, like in a parking lot or something?'

'On the street, right in front of his building.'

'And here I am railing on the man for not showing up. Kind of insensitive, isn't it? I've been told that I come off as insensitive.'

'Well, under the circumstances, it's understandable. It sounds as if Mr.

LaRoche could be a bit difficult.'

'That's an understatement. First time I worked with him. And it would have been the last time. Oops, there I go again, huh?'

Frank navigated through Roven's digressions to ask further questions. It appeared that LaRoche should have had his own set of papers with him as well. If he did, they must have been taken. It took two more circuitous trips around to the topic before Frank was satisfied that Roven knew of nobody close to LaRoche and had only dealt with him and his assistant. The seller of the property was a company called Bizel Financial.

There would be more questions, but he needed to explore more pressing items at the moment. He thanked Roven and said he would shortly be in touch again and would like to be able to see the documents relating to the sale.

As he hung up, he shook his head. All of this might or might not be germane. For all he knew, this was still a straight-up holdup gone bad.

He noticed two of the day-shift detectives, Leon Simpkins and Art Dowdy, standing next to Dowdy's desk, talking. He strolled over to them, everybody exchanging nods as he approached.

'Frank, what's up? Aren't you on the other shift this week?'

'Yeah. I just caught a shooting and had to follow up this morning. I'm about to head home. I just wanted to ask about something.'

They were a strikingly disparate pair. Simpkins was a tall, muscular outgoing African-American with a ready smile; Dowdy was short, lean, ash-blond and dour. Both were in their thirties. Some on the unit jokingly referred to them as the Emcée and the Mortician. Frank thought of them as Mutt and Jeff, the old comic-strip characters, but figured most of the younger guys would have no clue as to who they might be. Despite the jokes, he knew them both to be smart and aware. They looked at him expectantly. Dowdy drained the coffee cup he was holding.

'My vic got shot twice at close range in an apparent walk-up robbery. You guys caught anything like that lately?'

Simpkins folded his arms in thought,

then shook his head. 'Not really, no.' He looked to Dowdy for corroboration. His partner just shook his head. 'You're thinking it's a repeater?'

'Maybe somebody doing a string of quick swoops. Sounds like he walked up to the guy on the street and just plugged him. Emptied his pockets but left a watch. Might have grabbed up a briefcase as well.'

'Any witnesses?'

'One guy, not much help. Saw two guys bumping against each other and heard shots. He wasn't all that close. It was getting dark.'

They both shook their heads again. 'Not like anything we've caught of late.'

'I'm just hoping against hope that there's a pattern of some kind. This has the potential to . . . '

Just then, Frank's phone began to buzz in his pocket. He fished it out, flipping it open.

'Frank's still got that relic,' Dowdy said to his partner. Simpkins smiled back. They were two of the tech-savvy types on the unit that were his constant sparring partners. Frank just gave them a smirk and turned away.

'Vandegraf here.'

'Detective, it's Marielle Tarkenton. Mr. Jellicoe asked me to give you a call.'

'Yes, Ms. Tarkenton, what's up?'

'We might be able to help you find a next of kin. Mr. LaRoche left a will.'

'A will?'

'Yes, and there's a copy on file at the office.'

'That was good thinking, Ms. Tarkenton.'

'Actually Mr. Jellicoe thought of it. He told me to look it up and call you before you decided to come see him again. He also specified I should pass that along as well.'

'Salt of the earth, that man. Must be a joy to work for him.'

There was a brief pause and the slightest sigh. Clearly she was within hearing range of her boss, or thought she might be. Then she said, very business-like, 'I'll tell him you said thank you. I looked it over and there's only one name mentioned in it.'

'One name? He only remembered one person in his will?'

'He left everything to her. Her name is Sarah Hartnett and the address on the document is in Sycamore Creek.'

Sycamore Creek was a town about twenty miles east of the city, a somewhat upscale area where people who could afford to would flee when they tired of the big city. He hurried back to his desk and jotted down the specific address she gave him.

'What are the chances she's still there, do you think?'

'Well, he updated the will only last year, so I'd guess pretty good.'

'And you have no other information on this Sarah Hartnett or even know who she is?'

'I'm afraid not. I asked Mr. Jellicoe and he'd never heard of her.'

'I guess I'll have to go ask her myself then. Thanks for that. Please tell Mr. Jellicoe that I can't guarantee that he's seen the last of me, but his efforts are appreciated.'

As luck would have it, when he checked

online he found a Sarah Hartnett listed at the address. When he dialed the number it was picked up on the first ring. A voice both hoarse and nasal said, 'Hello?'

'Hello, I'm looking for Sarah Hartnett?'

The woman on the other end sneezed. 'And just who's this?'

'Police Detective Frank Vandegraf. Would this be Ms. Hartnett?'

She coughed. 'Yes, this is she. What's this about?'

'Ms. Hartnett, I'm calling about Julius LaRoche. Do you know him?'

'Do I know him?! What's up with Julie now?'

'Uh . . . Ms. Hartnett, I'm afraid something has happened. You're the only person I've been able to locate who might have some connection to him.'

She coughed again and cleared her throat. 'Something's happened? Did he give you my name or something? That would be a first.'

'I'm afraid he's been killed.'

'What? Are you kidding? Julie's dead?'

'Yes. He was killed last night.'

'Wow.' Another pause, this time with no

coughing or sneezing. 'I'm not sure how to react to that news, Detective.'

'Had you seen him or talked with him recently?'

'No. Not in a long time.'

'And how do you know Mr. LaRoche, exactly?'

'I'm his daughter.'

Estranged daughter, as Frank learned from the rest of their conversation. When she asked, he went into greater detail about the circumstances of his death. She was surprised but didn't seem particularly upset. He learned she had had no contact with her father since moving to Sycamore Creek a number of years earlier. The last she had spoken with him had been at his house.

'That was the house with his second wife. I was still living with my mother at the time. So you haven't been able to locate Dahlia then?'

'Dahlia?'

'The second Mrs. LaRoche, lucky woman. I understand she divorced him. Probably moved as far away from him as she could get.' Hartnett coughed again.

'Excuse me. I'm home from work with this cold or flu or whatever it is. Otherwise you wouldn't have reached me this morning. Excuse me again.' She blew her nose. 'So how did you get my number, exactly?'

'You're mentioned in his will, Ms. Hartnett. In fact you're the only one in it.'

That clearly took her aback. Another long pause.

'I'm in Julie's will?'

'Apparently he left everything to you.'

'Holy crud! Really? I can't believe it.' She blew her nose again. For a moment Frank had regretted breaking this news to her on the phone rather than in person, but given her attitude and her communicably diseased state, he was glad it had worked out this way. 'It's not like we were close, you know? I don't think we've even spoken in, like, six or seven years!'

'His law partner will be getting in touch with you about the will. I'm sorry for your loss.'

'I really have to process this. This is crazy. I'm sorry, I must seem terrible to you, not breaking up over the news that my father's dead.'

'Grief is a strange thing, Ms. Hartnett. Everybody reacts differently.'

'I mean, I didn't hate him or anything. I just sort of wrote him off, do you know? Wow.'

'Your mother was his first wife, is that correct?'

'Yes. She changed her name back to Hartnett and I did the same.'

'Is it possible to talk with her?'

'Do you know the line from the classic old movie, 'I think you'll find the conversation somewhat one-sided'?'

'*Casablanca*. Conrad Veidt. So you're telling me . . . ?'

'Yep, my mom passed away five years ago.'

'I'm sorry.'

'Thank you. She was pretty cool. She kinda got along with my father, even after he remarried. She was the one who encouraged me to keep contact with him and Dahlia.'

'And you don't know what happened to Dahlia?'

'No idea. She was a very sweet lady. Very patient, very accepting. I don't know what she saw in Julie. She and I got along really well, all things considered. When I stopped visiting them, I missed her a lot more than I missed him.'

'Why did you stop visiting them?'

'I was about sixteen. It was complicated. Some of it was issues with him. Some of it was just being sixteen, you know? Do you have kids, maybe teenaged kids?'

'No. But I have friends who do.'

'It's not an easy age. I was probably a self-absorbed pain, and I wasn't very understanding. We were fighting more and I finally just got sick of it and stormed out one day and never went back. I felt bad because Dahlia seemed really upset by our fighting. My mom tried half-heartedly to get me to reconcile for a while. But by then she was starting to get sick. She was sick for a long time.'

'I'm really sorry, Ms. Hartnett.'

She sneezed again. It sounded as if she was wiping off the phone receiver. 'It seems a long time ago, Detective . . . I'm sorry, what was your name again?'

'Vandegraf.'

'Detective Vandegraf. I've made my peace over my father. He did the best he could. He just wasn't a great husband or father. I've made a life for myself here in Sycamore Creek. I've got a good job, friends, a fiancé. All that other stuff is like history out of a book.'

'I'm still sorry to have brought you this news this way. I had no idea of your relation. I won't bother you any further right now. Maybe we can talk later, and if I can be of any help, please feel free to contact me.' He left her his office and cell phone numbers. 'One last question: do you think Dahlia would have taken back her original name after the divorce?'

'It makes sense. If it was anything like Julie's marriage to my mom, she would have wanted to get rid of his name as fast as she could. Her maiden name was Storm.'

'Dahlia Storm. Thank you, Ms. Hartnett. Again, I'm sorry.'

She started to laugh and it turned into a deep cough. Finally she said, 'My sorries happened a while ago, I guess. Time will tell.'

Frank shook his head as he hung up the phone. This guy left a wide swath of wreckage behind him. Was anybody going to miss him?

3

On his way in to the evening shift, Frank decided to drive by the so-called Bodega Building. There were still numerous people along the street and in the market and restaurant. Both looked to be very popular. He started with the market, Mercado Del Oso. He elbowed his way through the narrow aisles to the register, and was directed to the back of the store, where the owner, Felipe Del Oso, was busy with a clipboard inventory of some sort. He was a bear of a man, husky, over six feet tall, with dark curly hair and a thick dark beard. When he introduced himself and showed his badge, Del Oso put down his clipboard and flashed a huge grin.

'How can I help you, Detective? I'm Phil Del Oso, at your service.' He had a deep, resonant voice.

'Have you got a couple minutes, Mr. Del Oso?'

'Sure, c'mon over here.' He led Frank

through a door into a storage area filled with crates of mangoes, bananas, and other fruit. 'Sorry, we've got an office but we got a late delivery of fish and *some fool put it in the office!*'

He shouted the last part with a laugh back into the store, at a young man lifting boxes, who grinned back and said loudly, 'Hey, Pop, they had to go somewhere!'

'Anyway, plantains smell better. So here we are.' He reached for a rag on top of one of the stacks and wiped his hands. 'So what's up?'

'I wanted to talk to you about Julius LaRoche.'

'The guy who's buying the building? Is he complaining about us or something?'

'Are you aware that Mr. LaRoche was killed last night?'

'Killed? No way!' Del Oso seemed genuinely surprised. 'What happened?'

'It looks like a robbery. He was shot twice at close range.'

The man's eyes opened wide. 'The hell you say!'

'I understand he was about to buy this building and threatened to evict your market and the restaurant next door.'

'Yeah, he was gonna throw *everybody* out. You say he was 'about to' . . . does that mean he . . . ?'

'Yes, it would seem he was killed before he could complete the transaction. The sale never happened.'

Del Oso sighed deeply. 'I'm sorry it happened to him. But I have to admit, I've got what you call mixed feelings.'

'I also understand you had some words with Mr. La Roche over the impending purchase recently, in his office?'

'Ah. So that's what this is about. We had a discussion, yes. My son and I went to his office to try to work out something. This market is everything I've got. My family is invested in this. We decided we'd try to present a counter-offer, buy the building ourselves. The seller told us LaRoche had first rights and we needed to talk to him.'

'I assume Mr. LaRoche was not receptive to your overtures.'

'No. No, he was not. His whole attitude was basically it was a done deal and for me to deal with it.'

'So you argued?'

'That's not my way, Detective.' He smiled slightly through his thick beard. 'You know when there are serious diplomatic dealings and they describe then as 'frank talks'? That was what we had. Neither of us raised our voice. Nobody threatened anybody or said anything intemperate. We spoke seriously but respectfully. I made my points and left.'

'I don't think you were just going to leave it at that. What was your next move going to be?'

'We talked to a lawyer. We had a legal challenge in the works.'

'So he was racing to get the sale done before your challenge could go through, it seems. He was in a hurry to jam the transaction through.'

Del Oso shrugged. 'Could be. I don't know. I was afraid he'd be moving fast so we were trying to be just as fast. We were hoping to get a stay on it, build public opinion against it, maybe even get the building declared a historical landmark. I was supposed to talk to a reporter this week from one of the locals. She's been working on stories about LaRoche.'

Frank wondered if she might be the same reporter who had written about Julie's condo-conversion evictions. He made a note to follow up on that when he got the chance.

'You say your son accompanied you when you went to see LaRoche?'

'Yeah. Daniel's my second in command. Someday the mercado will be his . . . *if* we can keep it alive. I like to take him on my business calls, to wholesalers and such, so he can learn.' Del Oso stared intensely at Frank. 'Are you thinking this really wasn't a robbery like you told me, that this was like payback or a message kind of thing?'

It was Frank's turn to shrug. 'Right now I'm just trying to accumulate the facts, Mr. Del Oso.'

'But you're thinking maybe I had something to do with it, right?' His bright smile was now gone, replaced by a cold glare.

'I've got no theories. It does seem a lot of people had it in for him.'

'That wasn't a 'no' to my question, though.'

'Chances are it's exactly what it seems,

a holdup turned tragic. But when a guy's made as many enemies as he did, I have to investigate all the possibilities.'

'You can ask around about me all you want, Detective. You'll find I'm a straight guy, not somebody who would do something like this.'

Frank thought, but did not say, that in his experience everybody could have done something like this. That made his job a little harder and less pleasant, but there it was.

★ ★ ★

The small, bustling restaurant was called Rincon Guatemalteco. The proprietor was a short, stocky man who introduced himself as Oscar Argueta. He motioned Frank over to a tiny corner table and sat with him, looking attentive. They had to speak loudly over the tumult of the patrons. He was surprised to learn of the death of Julie LaRoche and shook his head sadly.

'I never knew the man. It's still sad to learn of anyone dying in this way. Did he have a family?'

'Not close. He was divorced. There's a surviving daughter.'

'A shame. How may I help you in this matter?'

'It's my understanding that he was about to buy the building and planned to evict the tenants.'

'Yes, there was word to that effect. It wouldn't have mattered to me. I hadn't mentioned this to anyone, but I planned to give my notice soon anyway. We found a larger location with an option to buy, and the rent was comparable. If anything, this might have worked for the best; I'm sure we could have negotiated out of the remaining months on our lease.'

'What about the other tenants in this building? I mean besides Felipe Del Oso's market. The people upstairs.'

'There's only a handful of apartments on those two upper floors, and they seem to be mostly vacant of late. I'm thinking the current owners were not renewing leases or re-renting. Perhaps they anticipated the sale of the building.' Argueta frowned. 'And as to what had been said to Felipe about his mercado, I don't have the slightest idea.'

Frank decided this was a dead end and thanked Argueta for his time.

* * *

Back at the station, Frank found manila envelopes on his desk: preliminary reports from the coroner and SID on the LaRoche case. It was still possible to get hard-copy results as well as to receive them by email, and while Frank was grudgingly coming around to reading them online, he still opted to receive printed reports he could hold in his hand. They were brief and, as expected, offered nothing new: two bullets in the victim, .38 caliber, residue consistent with both shots being fired into the chest at very close range. They came from a revolver; no shells were left at the scene. No other evidence on the body or clothing. No defensive wounds or signs of a struggle. The slugs had been sent to ballistics to check for matches to other crimes. If he was very lucky there'd be a match to an actual gun, but he knew it was unlikely.

There were also transcripts of the uniformed officers' reports. They were likewise inconclusive. Nothing had turned up that could have been connected to the victim.

If this were indeed a straightforward anonymous robbery, Frank saw little chance of any further breaks. There were numerous robberies of opportunity in the city every week, assailant unknown to victim. He had four others on his desk right now and he was spinning his wheels on all of them. Every now and then, somebody died in the commission of those robberies. That was probably what had happened in this case. His only chance was if there was more to the murder — if it were actually personal — but the odds against that were large, even given the animosity that Julie seemed to inspire in every part of his life.

He started perusing the papers that Marielle Tarkenton had copied for him. He read through the unsigned *Blade-Courier* editorial, a brief, reasonably restrained two paragraphs. It began by saying that the infamous Julius LaRoche had once again achieved an unspecified settlement in a liability suit against a convent of charitable nuns and went on to lament what it termed the 'litigation-drunk' state of current society. Frank didn't see any specific potential in that, but it did reinforce Julie's infamy as the most hated man in the city.

He turned to the article on the Webleyview conversion, written by a reporter named Lorena Park for a tabloid called the *Urban Sentinel*. The article, entitled 'Dumped on the Streets,' ran several pages, punctuated by photographs of unhappy-looking people standing in front of the controversial edifice, and referred to LaRoche as 'LaRoach' in several places. It was passionate writing, Frank decided, but hardly objective.

Park described several of the people who had lived for many years in the building before it had been bought and turned into Webleyview. Her elderly uncle and aunt, who had been immigrants from Korea and now lived with her own parents, were among those she profiled, along with three people she claimed had become homeless afterward. One of them had passed away not long before the article had been written. There was even a photograph of her gravesite. Park had miraculously succeeded in actually portraying Julie LaRoche in an even more negative light. Frank could imagine what the conversation must have been like when Park visited the law offices, and could imagine the litigation that Julie was planning. He figured it was worth a call to see if he could reach Lorena Park, even though it was getting late. He found the number for the *Urban Sentinel* and navigated a recorded directory through to her. He was surprised when she picked up on the first ring.

'This is Lorena Park,' she said in a voice that announced she would brook no foolishness. This was a no-nonsense woman, Frank mused. He identified himself to her and explained he was calling because of Julius LaRoche.

'I heard this afternoon about the shooting. How can I help you, Detective Vandegraf?'

Someone who got his name right on

the first try, he reflected. Good start. 'I see you wrote an article about him and I understand you were possibly following up on another one?'

'Correct on both counts. Are you thinking he was killed by someone he wronged? I was under the impression it was a robbery.'

'It's looking like that, but I'm just looking into everything.'

'Of course. It's not like he didn't have any enemies. You're probably getting that idea by now.'

'He did seem to have a way with making friends. How did you get interested in writing about him to begin with?'

'If you've read my article, you know when he bought Webleyview out from under all the tenants, that two of the people he displaced were my relatives. They're smart, wonderful people who came to this country and worked hard and did well. But they've gotten old and they're living on their pensions. When this happened to them and my parents had to take them in, I was outraged and started looking into it. Most of the people being dislocated were elderly, minorities, people on fixed incomes, in general powerless and unable to fight back. It's not exactly an upper-class neighborhood, but it's been stable for decades, until the forces of destabilization started coming in. When I discovered what kind of a manipulative bully Julius LaRoche is — or I guess I should say 'was' — I knew I had to write about him.'

'So you interviewed him for the article?'

'I tried. He put me off several times. Finally I went to his office and confronted him. That didn't go well. He never did offer any comment for the article. I went ahead and finished the piece and submitted it, mentioning that he had refused to be interviewed for the story.'

'I can't imagine it was well received in his office. Any reaction?'

'A couple of angry calls to the paper threatening to sue. My publisher is used to that. He offered LaRoche the opportunity to write a letter of rebuttal which he would print. I don't think the offer got taken up.'

'Conceivably he took offense to being called LaRoach, among other things.'

Park laughed. 'You think? The slimeball deserved it.'

'Forgive me, but it doesn't exactly seem an objective approach to the story.'

'It's called advocacy journalism, Detective. The *Sentinel* specializes in it.'

'And you were pursuing a new story on the proposed purchase of the Bodega Building?'

'I hate that name. That's what LaRoche was calling it, not anybody else. Once again marginalizing the people in the building and the neighborhood. Another attempt at destabilizing a vibrant and diverse community for his own profit. I especially hate what he had done to the Del Oso family, stealing the building out from under them like that.'

'I'm not sure I know what you mean, stealing the building? I thought it had recently been defaulted and he was buying it from the current owners?'

'You mean Bizel Financial. I guess you don't know how they got hold of the building to begin with, then?'

'Educate me, Ms. Park.'

'They specialize in refinancing mortgages. Let's just say they offer terms that might raise a few eyebrows. And if you look at their record, they have a suspiciously high rate of defaults and foreclosures.'

'This kind of stuff still goes on, even after all the scandals?'

'The owner should have known better. It's a complicated story that I'm still digging into for the details. The point here is that he refinanced and lost the building. And I guess you don't know that the victimized owner was Felipe Del Oso, huh?'

'Are you kidding me?'

'The things a reporter finds with her little shovel and spade, Detective.'

'So who is this Bizel Financial? Any connection with LaRoche?'

'That's one of the things I was looking for. It's shady and complicated, and the scum often rises to the top of pond all together. But as of yet I've found nothing.'

Frank was furiously writing on a legal

pad at his desk. His mind raced as he scribbled names and drew arrows and question marks to connect them. Del Oso had not mentioned anything about being the prior owner of the building. Argueta, who must have known, had not brought it up either. Nothing had been said about the possibility of Julie being in on the foreclosure and sale. Nothing pertaining to the transaction had been left at the office.

'This is fascinating stuff,' Park continued. 'But I'm not sure I'm seeing a connection to his death. I'm more thinking it was just his personal karma.'

'Excuse me?'

'The guy just attracted hostility. It would make more sense to me that a random mugger approached him and he gave the guy too much grief.'

'Not a conspiracy fan, then, I take it?'

'Oh, I love conspiracies. They're my bread and butter. But most of the time I'm disappointed when I go looking for them. It's usually the simplest solution, and that comes down to individual stupidity or venality rather than cabals.'

'Occam's Razor,' Frank offered.

'Yeah, sort of. Very good, Detective. You're a pretty sharp guy, you know?'

Frank rolled his eyes.

'For me, the real story is the building and how it was procured. It's a treat when I can actually uncover some kind of deep collusion, and this Bizel thing looks promising. I doubt it's connected to the murder, but your man LaRoche may or may not turn up involved in that. Keep an eye out for my story.'

Frank found himself writing 'Bizel Financial' on his legal pad and circling it over and over. It was tenuous, but so was everything else he had. He decided it couldn't hurt to call an investigator he knew in the Financial Crimes unit and ask if the name rang any bells. He caught him in the office and had a brief chat. Bizel was unfamiliar to the investigator but he promised to look into it and get back to Frank.

He continued to idly trace ink circles on the pad, around and around the word 'Bizel.' Finally he realized that was exactly what his brain was doing: making circles over and over the same territory. He wadded up the sheet of legal paper and tossed it into his wastebasket.

Maybe tomorrow, Friday, something would present itself.

★ ★ ★

'I'm starting to get the impression, Detective, that you are suspecting me of Mr. LaRoche's murder.'

Felipe Del Oso had a broad smile on his face as he said that. They were sitting in the market's cramped office, looking at each other over the piles of invoices and other papers covering the cluttered desk. Del Oso had his legs stretched out to the side and was leaning back in his chair.

'I'm just curious as to why, last time we talked, you left out the simple fact that you used to be the owner of this building. That's kind of unusual.'

'It just sort of didn't come up, that's all. By the way, the room still smells of fish, doesn't it? I apologize for that. I'm going to give Danny a piece of my mind for letting them bring that stuff up here.

Sea bass . . . great fish, we sell a ton of it, but it's definitely strong . . . I don't know what he was thinking.'

'No matter, Mr. Del Oso. So it's come up now. You owned the building and you . . . lost it?'

Del Oso's expression grew more serious now. His thick dark eyebrows knitted together low and he frowned through his beard. He sat forward and nodded. 'I needed money in a hurry. Unfortunately I felt a certain urgency and took out a loan on my equity from someone I probably shouldn't have.'

'So you're saying you couldn't go through a legitimate source.'

Del Oso hesitated and nodded.

'Are you going to tell me why you needed the money, Mr. Del Oso?'

It was a long moment before he considered and made his decision. 'My son got into some trouble. If he didn't pay certain people, there would have been unfortunate consequences.'

'Your son Daniel, who works here?'

'No, no. Not Danny. My younger son. Jesse. You're not going to see him working here. Not at the moment, anyway. At the moment he's kind of what you'd call the black sheep of the family. He's also far away from here right now.'

'What are we talking here? Gambling debt? Drugs?'

'Gambling. He was into them pretty deeply. By the time he came to me it was way out of hand. And with these guys, it grows by the day, if you get what I'm saying.'

'What did he owe when he came to you?'

'It was over a hundred thousand. So I went to talk to them. They gave me three days to come up with the money or . . . well, things were going to happen to Jesse.'

'So he tried to run?'

'He left town, yes. He was scared. But you don't run from these guys, Detective. You gotta know what I mean, right? You pay them. That's your only alternative.' Del Oso buried his head in his hands on the desk. 'I got problems with Jesse. He's the prodigal son, you know? But he's my son.'

Frank nodded. 'So you had to come up with a lot of money in a hurry.'

'The only thing I had to put up to get that kind of money was the building. And it had to be fast.'

'So you went to Bizel.'

'Yeah. In fact they were, shall we say, suggested, as a source of quick revenue by the holders of Jesse's debt.' Del Oso looked up and cast a long meaningful gaze at Frank. He got the point.

'So you paid off Jesse's debt in full, got guarantees he'd be safe?'

'As long as he stayed away from them from now on. I told Jesse not to come back, to stay far away, just to be sure of that. And he hasn't come back.'

'And the next thing you know, they're repossessing the building out from under you.'

'We had this building for quite a while. When we came to this neighborhood, it was considered 'depressed.' Lots of new immigrants, especially from Latin America. Property was cheap. I saw the real promise in this neighborhood. It's vibrant, lots of energy, lots of good people. I believed in them and took a chance, buying the building, opening the mercado, leasing to the restaurant. It was paying off.' He shook his head. 'And then this all happened.'

'How long ago was this, when they took over the building?'

'Maybe four months. But it didn't take long to see that so much was going to go down the drain. They were already driving away the tenants and emptying the building through attrition. It didn't take long.'

'So you were trying to buy back the building. But how were you going to do that?'

'I had time to arrange some more legitimate loans. From private sources, who wouldn't look at the forfeiture. They were people I couldn't go to with my original problem. This time I had to swallow my pride and explain the whole situation to them. Some of them came through for me. I could have swung it.'

'But the deck was stacked against you, wasn't it?'

'Oh yeah. The fix was in. There was no way I was gonna get it back.'

'When you went to talk to LaRoche . . . ?'

'I think that SOB had his hand in this. I think he was in bed with those *ladrónes* from the beginning.' Del Oso glared at Frank. 'So, now I guess, Mr. Policeman, that you're really convinced I had something to do with the murder of that worthless weasel?'

★   ★   ★

Friday evening was unusually quiet in the squad room, with only a handful of people around. It was almost funereal, compounding the heavy feeling on Frank as he sat at his desk, scratching out diagrams and notes on a legal pad. Some detectives preferred to lay everything out on a big white board in the conference room. He had become more comfortable with the intimacy of his legal pad.

In the center of the page he had written JULIE LAROCHE in large capitals, circled three times. Arrows radiated out to the peripheries of the paper, where he had jotted various other names and items. In one corner he had written BIZEL FINAN-CIAL and had drawn arrows (with question marks) to Julie, to MISSING BRIEFCASE?, to GAMBLERS, to JESSE DEL OSO, and to FELIPE DEL OSO. The whole group took up a good quarter of his page.

Jesse Del Oso was apparently a bad apple to begin with, but had truly overextended himself into a trouble zone with the gamblers. Maybe they had deliberately maneuvered him into that zone in order to get their hands on the Del Oso property. It was a digression that might perhaps interest the Organized Crime unit, but the only truly relevant factor was if it motivated Felipe Del Oso to kill LaRoche.

Could Julie LaRoche be directly involved in this? Frank couldn't see it that way. Felipe had been in plain sight, with witnesses and employees, in the market that entire evening. He could have hired someone to murder LaRoche, but somehow that didn't feel right either. His gut feeling was that Phil Del Oso was a straight-up guy. Straight-up guys had been known to commit crimes, even kill people. He'd have to keep exploring.

He could really stretch his imagination: Julie had been involved in the scheme; his co-conspirators had killed him and taken the documents to cover their tracks. The potential connections and schemes seemed endless, and they mostly struck him as groundless fantasies. His experience and logic persisted that it was exactly what it seemed, a random robbery turned homicide.

He had to admit he wanted this case to involve some kind of causal linearity, like a conspiracy or a crime of passion. Senseless crimes drove him crazy, not just because they were futile and unnecessary excursions ending in human tragedy, but because he wanted something logical and rational to explore and unwind. But the more he looked at it, the less that made sense. He could fight it all he wanted, but there it was.

He looked at the clock on the wall. One hour until his shift ended. He pulled out another legal pad, laid it next to the first, and dove back into his twisting diagrams.

4

Frank didn't make it to his desk Monday morning before being intercepted in front of Castillo's office and beckoned inside. The lieutenant actually gestured for Frank to have a seat.

'Frank, did you make some inquiries with Financial Crimes about a company called Bizel?'

'Yeah, actually, I did.'

'You're going to need to step back from that one. Leave it be.'

'I don't understand.'

'You couldn't have known, but you stepped into a hornet's nest. Bizel is apparently under deep investigation for money laundering or fraud or something, by a joint task force that includes the D.A.'s office and the FBI. Can't roil the waters or call attention to it.'

'You gotta be kidding me, Lou!'

'Straight from the captain. That, by the way, is just between you and me. Nobody else hears about this.'

Frank nodded and rubbed the back of his neck. 'That came out of nowhere, but I shouldn't be surprised, I guess.'

'I take it this has something to do with one of your current cases.'

'Possibly. It's a long shot, some background on the LaRoche murder. He was about to buy a building that might have been acquired by Bizel under some dubious circumstances.'

Castillo grunted a short laugh. 'Leave it to you to stumble onto something like that. But not overly germane to the murder, I take it?'

'I'd say it's a stretch. Interesting sidelight but I can't make a solid connection.'

'Then consider it a dead end. You're going to have to work around it. How's that case coming along?'

'I've got a city of potential suspects. Everybody hated him. His own law partner couldn't stand him. It's not like he was a connected guy; he was just a litigious, mercenary SOB. The killing may well be exactly what it looks like, a random act of violence in the commission of a robbery. I just wanted to take a peek at some things on the periphery. There's more of a chance of solving if it's not just a random attack.'

Castillo nodded. 'That's just like you, a thorough guy. I appreciate the due diligence, but don't get too caught up following red herrings. You know to follow the evidence and not get caught up in unsubstantiated theories.'

'I know. And I'm not neglecting the rest of my caseload. I just want to get what I can on this one while it's still warm.'

'And that's the other thing I called you in to tell you. You're getting a new partner.'

Frank took a deep breath. This was faster than he had expected. He hadn't had the chance to prepare himself. 'Lou, is this really necessary?'

'She comes highly recommended, Detective. It's time you stopped your solo act.'

'She?'

'Yeah, our new detective's a woman. Have you got a problem with that?'

'The woman part, hell no. Come on, Lou. You know me. One of the best detectives we have in Personal Crimes is Jilly Garvey. A couple of the sharpest unis I know are women . . . '

Castillo nodded, a wry smile actually sprouting under his thick mustache. 'Some of your best friends, you mean? Frank, you are digging yourself into a hole here, you know that? And I swear you're turning red, too, by the way.'

'No, honestly, I mean it. I might never have closed that weird parking lot murder last year without that Officer Pardo doing all the extra footwork, and . . . '

'Now that's interesting,' Castillo interjected, but Frank found himself continuing to babble.

' . . . it's just, you want me to babysit a brand-new baby?'

'You're worried we're getting a dud. And that the responsibility's going to fall on you. You're going to be wasting your precious time in training them.'

'Well . . . '

'Frank, would it help if I told you that our new promotion is up from the uniforms and she's proven herself to be bright, resourceful, and highly effective?'

'A uni? Not a transfer from Property or somewhere? That's a surprise.'

'Well, one of the things that influenced that decision was an absolutely glowing recommendation from one of our own detectives here.' Castillo stared at Frank and waited for the realization to dawn on him. 'And who better to break her in than her patron saint?'

'Pardo?'

'That's right.'

'Athena Pardo has been assigned to Personal Crimes?'

'She'll be here any time now. Think you can find her a desk out near you?'

Frank rose. 'Sure.'

He was halfway out the door when he almost collided with Athena Pardo. He nearly didn't recognize her with her hair down, in a blazer and slacks rather than a patrol officer's uniform, looking rather self-conscious. She had a cardboard box with some of her personal items. She gave him a startled smile.

'Detective Vandegraf.'

'Detective Pardo,' he replied. 'Welcome aboard.'

'Detective Pardo, come on in,' said Castillo. 'Frank's going to get you set up while we go over some things.'

Frank commandeered a nearby empty desk and was able to haul it over so it faced his own, then he rolled the accompanying chair over. He sat down and tried to follow his usual morning routine, jotting down notes and to-do items on his legal pad, but he found it difficult to concentrate. Before very long, Castillo walked Athena over to his desk and said, 'You're in good hands. Welcome to Personal Crimes,' and disappeared.

Frank looked up at Athena. 'Detective Vandegraf.' She smiled. She was trying to be confident, but he could detect a certain nervousness in her voice and manner.

'Detective Pardo.' He smiled back. 'I told you we'd be calling you that someday.'

'Yes, sir, you did,' she said, the hopeful smile still frozen on her face. She stood awkwardly, carton in her hands, waiting. Frank hated this uncomfortable ice-breaking nonsense. On a crime scene they would have been talking naturally, but now the situation was different.

'Forget the 'sir' stuff. I'm Frank and you're Athena, okay? As the lieutenant said, welcome to Personal Crimes.' He pointed with the pen in his hand to the empty desk. 'Stow your gear and let's get started.'

He gave her a quick tour around the unit, introducing her to various people, many of whom already knew her from the street. The reception was generally cordial but short. There was always some trepidation about a new detective, but Pardo had a good reputation as a smart but righteous cop. That would help her over the first few weeks. By the end of the morning, he had oriented her to the general routines of business. He regretted that his colleagues Jilly Garvey and Dan Lee were out on a case. He knew they'd be supportive — Jilly would no longer be the sole woman detective on the squad, and Dan hadn't had his detective shield all that long either. Frank had to confess to himself that he felt a little dubious about being able to be a strong enough support for his new partner. He had never broken in a newbie. He wasn't sure if he'd go about it the right way. He'd find out soon enough.

They grabbed a quick lunch and then concentrated on familiarizing her with the cases they'd be handling. As he had expected, she was a fast study. They sat at his desk while he gave her an overview of each of the cases and she nodded, asked the right questions, and made the right observations. This might work out okay. Things were just going to go more slowly while she absorbed the system and procedures, and they both learned to stay out of each other's way.

'Right now, I'm kind of a wheel-spinning mode. I guess now it's we are.' He picked up the stack of files and ceremoniously dropped them back on the desk with a thump.

'So you're mostly re-canvassing, follow-ing up with witnesses, that type of thing?'

'Exactly. I hate to do this to you in your first week, but we have to wade through some of this garbage and try to close some of these.'

'No problem,' said Athena, picking up one of the files and leafing through it. 'Sounds like a good way to get my feet wet, in fact. How about this one?'

Frank shrugged. 'They all gotta get done. Take your pick.'

'So,' Athena said as she perused the reports in the file, 'this is the lunch-counter operator that got mugged.'

'Yeah, Garo's Café, over on Goff. Older guy runs the place. Business district, only open for breakfast and lunch until mid-afternoon. He was closing up when two guys entered and beat and robbed him. He was in the hospital for a few days with a concussion. When I finally got to talk to him he didn't remember much. Couldn't ID the assailants. They were masked. No other witnesses.'

'I see he has a daughter who was there.'

'She was lucky; she was in the back in the kitchen. She hid under a table until she heard them leave. She didn't see anything.'

'And no other employees.'

'He's got a kitchen guy who leaves early. Same for a couple of waitresses. His afternoons get slow, so it's usually just him and the daughter for the last hour or so.'

'Nobody on the street saw anything?'

'Nobody came forward. It's a business district: financial offices, banks, law offices and such. There wouldn't be much foot traffic to speak of for another hour or so. The perps likely knew that when they picked their time and place.'

Athena nodded, still reading. 'No luck with canvasses, no cameras?'

'I had unis checking up and down and I was out there too. A couple security cams but nothing to be found. These guys seem to have scoped out the venue pretty well.'

'So maybe they're locals.'

'Very possibly. They might even come in to eat there. No luck on that angle either.'

'How's the victim doing?'

'He recovered, more or less. He's back at work.'

'Okay, then.' She packed up the file and slid it under her arm.

'It might be easier to follow up by phone.'

'If you don't mind, I'd like to do this in person, get a better handle on it.'

Frank hesitated. He wasn't sure how he was supposed to handle this. 'I'm thinking Castillo expects me to hang out with you the first day or two at least.'

'Detective — I mean Frank — I appreciate that but it's not like I've never done follow-up interviews as a patrol officer, you know? This is pretty routine, isn't it?'

Frank shrugged. 'Okay, go for it.' He picked up another file and hefted it as if it weighed a ton. 'I'm going to start making the follow-up calls on this one. Same story. Too many cases going nowhere until we find something new.'

Pardo smiled slightly. 'You've got an extra pair of eyes and legs now.'

'And they're appreciated. When you're done, head back here and we'll go over the LaRoche case together.' He waved the file as if he had won the jackpot. 'I definitely need a fresh viewpoint on that one.'

★ ★ ★

Garo Bedrosian hardly seemed thrilled at the prospect of the department's continuing interest in his case. When Athena arrived around two thirty and showed her ID to the stocky and weary-looking man behind the counter, he finished pouring a cup of coffee for his lone patron at the counter and muttered, 'So now they come back. And this time they send a girl.'

She let the comment go. Nothing she hadn't heard before. 'Detective Pardo, Mr. Bedrosian. Do you have a few minutes for me to ask you some more questions?'

Bedrosian grabbed a towel and began wiping down a stretch of the counter. 'Two weeks and nothing. What do you expect to happen, talking to me now?'

'We've been trying, sir, but frankly we just haven't had that much to go on. We thought maybe going over everything with you again, something might turn up we missed the first time.'

Bedrosian stopped wiping and looked up at her with impossibly tired eyes. 'We, you say. Who's this 'we'?' He gestured at her. 'I see you.'

'You remember Detective Vandegraf. I'm his partner.'

Bedrosian shrugged. 'So now he's got a partner. A girl partner. Okay, partner, come on down here and ask me your questions.' He nodded his head to the end of the counter. It was a small narrow lunch room, a counter with a dozen seats and three small tables up against the window. As they walked to the end of the counter, the swinging door to the kitchen opened behind Bedrosian and a thin dark-haired young woman came out.

'Cecy, keep an eye on the customer, will you?' he said to her. 'I need to talk to this policewoman here for a minute.' The young woman nodded and headed towards the coffee and soft-drink dispensers. The customer, shaking his head as she lifted the coffee pot, made a gesture to request the check.

'Detective, actually, sir,' said Athena.

'Whatever. Whatever you like. Detective. So what can I tell you I didn't already? Doesn't sound as if you've had any of what you like to call progress, am I right?'

Athena sighed. 'Maybe if we could just

go over what happened one more time . . . '
She pulled out her notebook and flipped it open.

Bedrosian sighed as if his patience were being taxed horribly. 'I was closing up the place. I must not have locked the door completely. These two guys entered, pulled out guns.'

'And that would have been . . . ' She consulted the notebook. 'Two weeks ago Tuesday. About three o'clock in the afternoon?'

'That's right. We do breakfast and lunch trade, mostly the banks and offices in the neighborhood. No dinner business here. Maybe some stragglers in early afternoon, late lunchers, people needing some coffee and sugar to get through the end of the day. I open at six and close at three.'

'Who was here at closing time?'

'Just me and my daughter, Cecilia.' He gestured over to her as she left the customer's check on the counter.

'I think I'd also like to talk with her as well.'

'Why? She was in the back when it all happened.'

'Still . . . '

Bedrosian shrugged again. 'Cecy, when you're done, please.' He motioned for her to come join them.

'So you were saying,' Athena resumed. 'Just you and Cecilia and the two men came in.'

'I was busy trying to get everything done so we could leave. Doing like five things at once.'

'And where were you at that time?'

Bedrosian pointed to the cash register, where his daughter was ringing up the sale. 'Right over there, by the register. I was about to empty the drawers and count the money before putting it in the bag for the night deposit. I had my back to the door. I figured I'd locked it. I heard it open and turned around.' He pointed to the door. 'There they were. They had jackets and, like, ski masks over their heads? And they had guns out. Pointed right at me.'

'What kind of guns, sir?'

'I don't know from guns. Pistols of some kind.'

'Revolvers? Automatics?'

'I don't remember. They had guns. They looked plenty scary to me. My first thought was Cecy. I thought she'd gone into the kitchen, but I didn't want to look around and let on there was anyone else in the restaurant. But I got good, whattaya call it, peripheral vision. I could tell she wasn't out here, so I hoped she'd stay in the back.'

'Their faces were covered, right? Could you see hands, eyes, anything?'

'The masks showed their eyes and their mouths. One guy maybe had like a beard or stubble or something. Don't remember the hands. Maybe they had gloves. A time like that, you don't think too straight.'

'I understand. How about the eyes? Remember anything about them?'

Bedrosian thought for a moment and shook his head. 'If I did see anything, you gotta realize, my memory isn't real good after what happened.'

Athena nodded. 'Just whatever you do remember, Mr. Bedrosian. Take your time. So they came in, then what? Did they close the door behind them?'

'They must have. I don't remember.

Wait . . . yeah. The sound. Open and then shut.'

'Was there anyone on the street going by?'

'I don't know. Probably not.'

'Could there have been another guy that stayed outside, kept watch?'

'No idea. There coulda been an army out there for all I know.'

'Okay. So . . . then what?'

'I just kinda froze there, taking it all in. The front guy yelled at me to be quiet, not to move or say anything unless they said to. Then he said to open the register. So I turned around and opened the register. One of them came around behind the counter and pushed me aside and started scooping up the bills out of the register. He asked if there was any more money. I said no, that was everything from the entire day. I was praying to myself that they didn't decide to search the back. But they didn't. They seemed nervous, in a hurry. The guy next to me gave me a look. It was scary. For a moment I thought he might shoot me.'

'You looked into his eyes then?'

Bedrosian nodded slowly. 'Yeah. Yeah. You know . . . I did see his eyes. I remember thinking they looked almost clear. They were gray.' He stopped for a moment. 'I did see his eyes. I had forgotten.'

'How about his voice, do you recall anything about it?'

'He kind of growled. I thought maybe he was purposely trying to sound gruff. Like he wanted to be scary. He was.'

'Mr. Bedrosian, you said he scooped up the money. What did he put it in?'

'I don't remember. Maybe he had a bag. Or stuffed it in his pockets. I just can't remember.'

'Then what?'

'He told me to turn around, to stop looking at him. The other guy said something to him about hurrying up, they had to get out. The first guy hit me across the back of my head. Hard. He hit me more than once. That's all I remember. Next thing I knew, Cecy was looking down at me, looking really worried, saying the paramedics were coming. It was all confused. Nothing made much

111

sense for a while until I found myself in the hospital.'

'You were in the emergency room with a concussion and internal head bleeding.'

Bedrosian nodded. 'Yeah. It all kinda ran together for a few days. It still does, now and then.' He kept shaking his head, looking down at his hands on the counter.

The customer had departed. Cecilia closed and locked the door and walked over to join them. Bedrosian smiled and placed a hand on his daughter's shoulder. 'Thank heaven she's here. It's taking me a long time to get right again.'

She looked at Athena expectantly, with large dark eyes full of concern. Things had not gotten right again here. Maybe they never would.

'Ms. Bedrosian, your father says you were in the back of the café the whole time the robbery was going on. Is that right?'

She nodded, casting an eye at her father. 'Yeah. It's my job to straighten up whatever's left in the kitchen at day's end.'

'Did you hear the robbers enter?'

'I heard the door open and slam shut.

My first thought was, we hadn't locked the door and there was a customer. Then I heard the voices.'

'You could hear what they were saying?'

'Oh yeah. They were shouting and angry. I got scared and hid under the sink back there.'

'You must have been worried about your father out there.'

Bedrosian interrupted. 'She did exactly the right thing. There's nothing she could have done by coming out with us. I was praying she'd do just what she did, hide back there.'

'Forgive me, Mr. Bedrosian. I wasn't suggesting otherwise. But . . . ' She turned back to Cecilia. 'You must have thought about doing something. Did you do anything before you went to hide under the sink?'

Cecilia looked very perturbed. She shook her head. 'No. No, I just . . . ran and hid.'

Athena noticed that Cecilia was not looking her in the eye anymore. 'You didn't look out the window of the kitchen door, or through the hand-through window over there?'

'No. No. I was too scared. I just hid.'

'And you could hear at least one of their voices?'

'Yes. I heard them both, yelling. It was really scary.'

'Do you remember anything about their voices, what they sounded like?'

'They were deep. Harsh.'

'What do you remember after that?'

'I heard them yelling at my dad. Then there were some other noises, they yelled some more, and I heard the door slam again. I waited under there for a long time. I was afraid one of them might still be out there, waiting to see if anyone else was there. I wanted to go check on my dad, but I was so scared . . . ' She looked as if she might cry. 'Finally I knew I had to take a chance. I went out slowly and looked around, and I found my dad lying on the floor behind the counter.' She pointed towards the register. 'Over there.'

Athena simply nodded and waited. After a long moment, Cecilia resumed. 'I ran over and checked to see if he was okay. He wasn't conscious. So I went to

114

the phone and called 911.'

'And then you just waited with him?'

'I didn't know what else to do. I don't know how to do that CPR stuff but he was breathing, he just wasn't conscious. I sat with him and kept talking to him. He would make noises and stir now and then. I kept telling him to hang on, help was coming.'

Athena stood up. 'Let's take a walk around. You can show me where you were when everything happened, okay?' She walked to the register, followed by both of them. 'And the only thing they took was the money out of here, correct?'

'As far as I know,' said Bedrosian. 'Nothing else to take, really.'

'And how much did they get?'

'It was our busiest day of the week. I'd left the cash from the previous day in there as well. There had to be close to a couple thousand dollars.'

'Is it usual for you to leave money overnight?'

Bedrosian looked sheepish. 'Yeah. I'd been getting kind of lax. Just easier to bag it up every couple days and take it to the bank deposit. The neighborhood's good. I've never worried. I guess I learned my lesson the hard way.'

Athena carefully examined up and down the counter and the rest of the lunchroom. 'Can I see the kitchen?'

It was a small but tidy back area: prep table, grill, refrigerator, sink. Not much room to navigate around. There were storage cabinets under the table and grill and a small dark crawl space beneath the sink. 'You hid under there?' Athena asked, pointing. Cecilia nodded. She still couldn't look at Athena directly.

There was something, Athena decided.

She took a long look around, running her hand over some of the surfaces, judging spaces and distances. She walked to the pass-through window where a cook could hand out orders to be picked up. The Bedrosians simply watched and waited, looking impatient.

'You were in the hospital for how long, sir?' she finally asked.

'Eight days. Cecy and the crew kept the place open. It wasn't easy.' He looked at his daughter with a proud smile. 'She was here every day, early to late. We would have gone under if not for her.'

'You must have been worried about her after what happened.'

'I was kinda not very responsive for a few days or I would have told her no. But she insisted on keeping our doors open. She's a brave girl.'

Cecilia looked embarrassed. 'I made sure Curtis was here with me. He's a pretty big guy. And Rosie and Yolie. We all pitched in.'

'So I finally come to and find out that they've been keeping the place going. What a family, this place.'

'It seems you came back to work pretty quickly yourself. Was that wise?'

Cecilia looked at her father with extreme concern. He waved his hands in dismissal. 'I was needed. I'm not a hundred percent, but I'm okay.'

'You must have been hesitant to return. That was a traumatic incident. It's not unusual for a victim of a violent robbery to feel apprehensive for some time afterward.'

'I've been in fights, worse than that. My

big concern was for my daughter and my people. But they all keep telling me they're not afraid.'

'Have you considered hiring a security guard?'

'Young lady, this could have happened anywhere to anyone. I've been here for twenty years and this is the first time such a thing has occurred. I'm not going to let it spook me. And besides, we can't afford a security guard. Especially after losing so much. I've got responsibilities to pay the people I've got already.'

Athena nodded. 'I think that ought to do it.' She turned to the door that led out of the kitchen. Bedrosian took the hint and led them out to the front.

Her business cards had not yet arrived, but she didn't want to have to explain that her detective shield was brand new, so she had come prepared. In her jacket pocket were several blank cards upon which she had written her cell number, and she now handed one to each of them. She asked them to call her if they could provide any further information whatsoever and tried to reassure them that she

and her partner were energetically following the case. Bedrosian nodded wearily
through it all, clearly not buying any of it.

As Athena put her hand on the
doorknob, she paused. 'Mr. Bedrosian,
how do you lock this door?'

'What do you mean?'

'The night of the robbery, can you just
run me through exactly what you did to
lock up, what might have been different
about that night?'

Bedrosian didn't respond at first until
Athena coaxed him further, asking him with
a self-effacing smile to humor her. He
sighed and walked to the door and started
to grab the knob and the lock mechanism
above the knob, then stopped, his expression blank. He simply stood there, looking
down at his hands for a long moment.

'Mr. Bedrosian?'

'I don't remember,' he said quietly.
'What I always do is to turn these locks
and . . . ' He went silent for several beats.
Then he shook his head, looking confused. 'I don't remember. It's a blank.'

'It's okay. Head injuries often affect
short-term memory, especially from the

time of the trauma. It's not important; I was just wondering. Thanks again. We'll be in touch to keep you up to date on progress.'

'Progress,' scoffed Bedrosian. 'Sure. Thank you, Officer.'

'It's Detective, actually.' She forced herself to smile, then turned to look at Cecilia. This time Cecilia was staring at her with an odd expression on her face. She sensed there was something here. She had to figure out a way to talk to her alone. That wasn't going to happen with her father hovering protectively over her. 'Hey, as long as I'm here, I keep hearing about someplace around that sells knock-offs of designer bags and accessories really inexpensively. I thought I might check it out while I'm in the neighbor-hood. Would you know the place?'

He shook his head. 'No, I don't know anything about that kind of stuff. Sorry.'

'I know the place you mean,' Cecilia said. 'I can show you where it is.' She walked to the door.

'That'd be great. Thanks.' Athena opened the door and left, followed by

Cecilia. 'And thank you again, Mr. Bedrosian, for your time.'

They stood on the sidewalk in front of the café and Cecilia pointed down the street. 'The next block down, see the building with the blue awnings? Their offices are one flight upstairs. It's called Latest Look Imports. No signs downstairs. You sort of have to know that it's there. I hear they've got bags that look just like the real thing at about a third of the price.'

Athena looked at Cecilia. The girl had that same expression on her face. 'If you don't mind my saying, you look like you need to talk to somebody. It might help to talk to me.'

Now she looked as if she might break out in tears. Athena waited. The words came slowly. 'I think it's my fault, what happened. You can't tell him.'

'What is it you think you did?'

Cecilia waited a long time, considering if she should could continue and what to say. 'My father wasn't the one who locked the door that night. He doesn't remember, probably because of the head injury.

It was me. I locked up that night. I must have not turned the lock all the way. It was still open when they came.'

'You're saying you left the door open?'

'I must have. It was an accident. You can't tell him. He can't know!' Her eyes grew wide and her lips set tightly, but she didn't cry.

'And you don't remember seeing anybody on the street outside when you were closing up?'

Cecilia shook her head. 'No, nobody. I'm scared to death he'll find out. It was my fault he got put in the hospital. He could have . . . '

Athena nodded. It didn't have to be said. Sometimes they died.

She looked back through the window of the restaurant, where Bedrosian stood watching them, hands on hips, waiting for his daughter to return. 'You've got my card. Give me a call if you want to talk some more, okay?'

As Cecilia turned to the entrance, Athena said, 'And I'd suggest you might want to stay away from Latest Look, okay? What they're doing there is illegal.'

In fact, she happened to know but wasn't about to say. It was on the department's radar for a number of reasons, and was ripe for an official visit any day now.

5

'So like I said, I don't have anything new to help you, Detective, but I appreciate your calling to assure me that absolutely no progress has been made in finding my attacker or my valuables.' Victoria Jasmine's voice on the other end of the line was throaty and brusque.

'It's not true that there's been no progress, Ms. Jasmine. These things take time, especially if it was a random crime of opportunity. I had hoped he might have had some connection to you. Maybe he had encountered you somewhere . . . something however small you might have remembered in the meantime . . . '

'As I just finished telling you, I'm sorry, I can't help you. I was walking to my car and the SOB pushed me into an alley against a wall, told me not to make a sound, and cut my purse strap and ran off with it. That's it.' There was a deep irritated sigh. 'Except that ever since, I feel like he's going to come back, and I can't get comfortable anywhere. I'm looking over my shoulder constantly . . . '

Frank listened patiently. It was the third time she had run through the exact same litany. Despite her sarcasm, it was clear that the crime had traumatized her deeply. He was frustrated but could only imagine how much worse she was feeling it.

' . . . yadda, yadda, yadda. Now is this the part where you tell me you're definitely going to find the guy?'

'I'm not giving up, Ms. Jasmine.' That was the best he could give her. He was always tempted to assure them he would definitely find their assailant, but he knew it was a lie. He wanted to once again remind her she had done the right thing by following the mugger's orders, that she was fortunate to have survived the attack, that sometimes the victims like her didn't make it. He had already told her that many times.

'Yeah, so you say. Let me know if anything breaks, as you guys say.'

'I'll keep you apprised. Don't hesitate

to call if you come up with anything, however inconsequential you think it might be.'

Wearily, he hung up and consulted his open notebook for the next telephone number to dial.

Athena noticed that Frank, hunched over his desk, didn't look very happy as she approached. He was just hanging up his phone and looked up to nod to her.

'How'd your follow-up go?'

She pulled over a chair and sat across from him. 'Interesting.'

Frank's eyebrows shot up. 'Let me hear, partner.' He stopped and shook his head.

'What's wrong, Frank?'

'Sorry. I just haven't said that in a long time. I'll get used to it. So fill me in.'

Frank listened as Athena recounted the interview. He had to admit being impressed. There might be something to the idea of another pair of eyes and ears on a case.

'I've got a feeling there's more to it than what she's telling me,' she concluded.

'You think she knows something? You think she's involved in it?'

'I don't know if I'd go that far. But she's got something we need to know, that's all I'm thinking.'

'Sounds to me like you've got good instincts, Athena. I'd trust them.'

'Hopefully I — we — can have the opportunity to talk to her outside of the shop. I don't know that it would do much good, but it'd be worth a try.'

Frank nodded. 'If that's your gut, we should go for it. You should go for it. She seems to be willing to open up to you. She didn't seem all that receptive to me at the time. Maybe I remind her of her dad.'

'How'd you do on that other case?'

'Spinning my wheels. How about we talk about the LaRoche murder?'

'Sure. What's our next move there?'

'You were on the ground with the unis that night. Maybe there's something I haven't heard. Fill me in on that.'

'Not much to tell. We covered the area for a few blocks around in case any of the victim's belongings had been dropped. We looked for wallet, briefcase, loose IDs, anything. Nothing found in the trash cans, gutters, alleys. We scoured for witnesses who might have seen the perp pass them, talked to bus drivers, cab drivers. No luck. I'm sure you saw the reports.'

'I did.'

'Only two pawnshop-type businesses in the immediate area. That was a long shot considering his watch and ring hadn't been taken, but maybe there was something else of value in his pockets that hadn't been accounted for. Nothing had been brought in.'

'We've got no way of knowing what he might have been carrying. No idea how much money he might have had in his wallet, or what else. I ran a search and could only find two credit cards in his name, one of which was his ATM card as well. He hadn't run credit in months and only used the ATM now and then. So far neither card has shown any activity since the robbery. He might have had a briefcase or a courier bag of some kind; he was apparently bringing documents to the escrow office. But nobody has been able to confirm anything.'

'A smart robber would try those cards immediately, before the word got out. Sounds as if he wanted cash . . . or hoped for something else of value. Maybe he figured, just an easy mark coming out of that building late.'

'Why not just rob him? Why kill him?'

'Maybe something went bad? Maybe the guy was overly nervous. Maybe he was jacked up on something. Maybe LaRoche resisted . . . just made the wrong move or said the wrong thing. It happens all the time, doesn't it? His death could have been totally unnecessary.'

'Yeah,' Frank replied slowly.

'What?'

'The thing is, you're probably right. I just can't shake the alternative scenario, that it was one of the dozens who held a grudge against him.'

'I could be wrong. It just feels like a random crime to me. But I'll trust your experience. So where do we go from here?'

★ ★ ★

Daniel Del Oso was a younger image of his father: dark haired and big-framed, though less stocky and with a stubblier beard. He was in the alley at the store's dumpster, tossing a few empty crates that still reeked of fish, when he heard the voice behind him.

'I sure hope you didn't put those in the office this time.'

He turned to the two people a few steps away and laughed. 'You're the cop who was here the other day, right? Pop's still giving me grief about that.'

'That's me. This is my partner, Detective Pardo.'

Daniel nodded at Athena and wiped his hands on his jeans. 'He's inside if you need to talk to him. You can come in the back door with me.'

'Actually we were hoping to talk to you, Daniel, if you've got a minute?'

'Sure, a minute. Then he's gonna ream me out if I don't get back to work.'

'Your dad works hard, and I guess he expects everyone else to do the same, right?'

'You got that right. He's a good man. A

damned good man.' He stared at them pointedly.

Frank nodded. 'Daniel, I know he couldn't have committed the crime we're investigating. He was working here last Wednesday night.'

'That's right. He's always here.'

'But here's the thing, Daniel ... ' Frank remembered an old television mystery show that his former wife had loved, featuring a police detective who was far craftier than the bumbling character he gave the impression of being. He would often pause at a crucial moment while interrogating a suspect and suddenly say, 'But there's this one thing I don't understand, maybe you can help me ... ' He couldn't help feeling he was taking a page from that character right now. Daniel waited for Frank to finish his sentence.

'Here's the thing ... I was wondering where *you* were on Wednesday evening, because nobody seems to be able to confirm that you were working here with him.'

Daniel looked bewildered. He raised

his hands, palms up. 'What do you mean? No, I wasn't working last Wednesday. I took the night off.'

'So . . . you were, where? At home? With friends? This is just routine stuff, to get you out of any conceivable doubt if somebody comes along and asks, you know? You must have been with somebody who can vouch for your whereabouts, right?'

'Actually, no. I was . . . oh hell, I was with a woman.'

'Okay. Your girlfriend? What's her name? Can we just talk to her? Just to, you know, dot the I's and all that?'

'Uh, no. Honestly, I don't know her name. Not her real name. She's, well . . . this is really embarrassing.' He shot a glance at Athena and back to Frank. 'Look, you can't tell my father, okay?'

Frank nodded in understanding and clapped a hand on the young man's shoulder. He hoped it was a fatherly gesture, or at least a conspiratorial one. 'Yeah. I can see this is kind of a bad situation.' He looked at Athena. 'Would you excuse us for just a second?' He led Daniel a dozen steps down the alley.

Athena, taken by surprise, shot him a sharp look and stood with her arms folded as they walked away.

'Daniel, I still have to do my job,' said Frank in a low voice. 'So you were with a . . . temporary companion, let's say. Just tell me who she is or where I can find her and this will be the last we speak of this, okay?'

'I don't know her name. She called herself Candy. Or Mandy or something like that. She's a dancer at one of those clubs along that strip a few blocks from here?'

'The district they call the Prime, you mean? Which place?'

'I don't remember. I was drinking.'

'Daniel, you're not helping me here. Is this something you do often?'

'Never. Honest. I was just a little crazy that night. Most of my friends work at the market or were busy. I don't have a girlfriend right now. I wandered into this joint, had a few drinks, and this girl offered some *special* dances, one on one in the back room? It just . . . seemed like a good idea at the time.'

It was kind of amusing. Daniel was a big guy but he was acting like a guileless teenager. 'So you're telling me the only person who can vouch for where you were on Wednesday is a mysterious exotic dancer named Candy or Mandy, at any one of a number of sleazy joints. Daniel, how can I help you if you make it so hard?'

'I'm sorry. It's the best I can do.'

'Can you at least describe her for me?'

'Dark hair. And, well, nicely built. That's all I remember.' Daniel stepped away from Frank. 'I gotta get back in now.'

Frank walked towards the mouth of the alley, joining Athena partway.

'I can't believe you did that.'

'Sorry. The kid's obviously been raised old school. He was embarrassed to talk about getting a lap dance in front of you.'

Athena chewed that over for a moment as they walked. Then she nodded. 'You're right. Just like Cecilia Bedrosian wouldn't have talked to you. This is about getting them to open up, playing to each other's strengths, right?'

Frank laughed. 'Louie, I think this is the beginning of a beautiful friendship.'

Athena stared at him. 'Who the blazes is Louie?'

'Claude Rains in *Casablanca*. Oh, never mind. You are young, aren't you? I'm going to have to introduce you to a classic film or two one of these days.'

★ ★ ★

None of the four clubs along the block nicknamed the Prime were yet open for business, but there were managers or staff on the premises. In all, there were four women using the name Candy, Brandy, Mandy and Randi that had been dancing the previous Wednesday. All of them were said to have 'darkish' hair and presumably all of them were 'nicely built.' None of them were currently available. Every single employee expressed shocked outrage at the very suggestion that any kind of inappropriate, much less illegal, services might be solicited at their establishment. Nobody could officially remember a patron meeting Daniel Del Oso's specific description. The entire neighborhood was one huge stonewall to them. They basically got nowhere.

On the walk back to their car, Frank muttered, 'It's not going to be worth coming back for this. Nobody's going to remember anything for us.'

'You seem really interested in Daniel Del Oso.'

'It's a possibility. I don't think Felipe was behind it — not directly, at any rate.'

'But you like the Del Oso clan in general? You seem to be pushing this.'

'I don't know, Athena. It's just something I need to clear up or I'm not going to feel comfortable.'

'Maybe Del Oso senior gets his son to do the dirty work, is that what you're thinking?'

'What I'm thinking is this is a wild goose chase. Daniel was never here and never with a girl named Candy or Sandy or whoever. He knew this would be too obscure to confirm or deny and that we'd just be wasting our time.'

'Meaning he was involved in this in some way?'

Frank raised his eyebrows as he opened

the car door. 'It would seem to indicate he's involved in *something* he'd rather we didn't find out.'

6

Frank arrived early Tuesday, resolved to catch up on some of the loose ends of the LaRoche case that still nagged at him. The first thing he decided to do was to track down Dahlia Storm, Julie's second wife.

He booted up his computer and began by tracing divorce records. He was proud of himself that it only took a few minutes to locate the documentation he needed. Dahlia and Julie had indeed finalized their divorce almost ten years ago. The records actually gave a new address for Dahlia since she had already moved out and adopted her maiden name once again. Did they still call it a 'maiden' name, Frank wondered, or would he offend someone by using that term today? He had no idea. No matter; if his arms were longer, he would have patted himself on the back. He was rolling now. He ran several more searches, each time gleaning some new piece of information. He found a Dahlia Storm listed in the directory of Last Hope, a non-profit legal aid agency that specialized in indigents and seemingly hopeless cases. How perfect, Frank mused. A reaction to Julie, perhaps?

He dialed the agency's number from their website. Despite the early hour, a receptionist picked up almost immediately. Frank identified himself and explained he was trying to locate Dahlia Storm.

'Oh dear,' said the woman on the other end of the line. 'Can you hold for just a moment please?'

He was only on hold about twenty seconds before a deep-voiced man picked up and said, 'I understand you're asking about Dahlia Storm?'

'Yes, that's correct. This is Detective Vandegraf from the Personal Crimes unit. I found her name on your agency directory. Is she still working there?'

There was a short pause. 'We do need to update that directory. I'm afraid Ms. Storm is no longer with us.'

'You mean she moved on to another job? Do you have any information of where she might — '

'No, no, Detective, I mean she *left* us. She is literally no longer with us. I'm sorry to have to be the one to tell you this. About seven months ago, she suffered a seizure at work. She was rushed to the hospital and they performed emergency surgery.'

Frank took a deep breath and waited for the punch line.

'There were complications. Dahlia unfortunately died on the table.'

Dahlia's death was a true dead end. She had listed no next of kin and had left everything in her will to Last Hope.

* * *

Tuesday morning, Athena could see, did not seem to be going well. Frank seemed clearly agitated as he scribbled on his legal pad at this desk. Since arriving for work, she had felt like she needed to avoid him, but now, a half hour later, she decided to approach him. He didn't look up.

She noted a short printout report on his desk, in large type, that stated that the slugs found in Julius LaRoche did not yield a match to any known weapon. There were several wadded-up sheets of legal paper strewn around the desk.

'I think we need to go back and give Daniel another shot,' he muttered, still staring at his desk.

'If that's what you want,' she said quietly.

Frank finally looked up. 'What?'

'What do you mean, what?'

'What's on your mind, is what I mean.'

'Not my place. If you want to talk to Daniel again, let's go.'

'Wait a minute. What's this nonsense, 'not your place'? If you've got something on your mind, you tell me. That's how this works.'

For a moment Athena considered what to say before Frank continued.

'It sounds as if I've been rubbing you the wrong way. I'm probably difficult that way. But I really want this to work. They could have assigned you to a goldbrick like Morrison, or I could have ended up with someone who doesn't know what they're doing. It's just that I haven't had a partner in a long time . . . '

'I know. You keep telling me that.'

Frank shook his head. The background noise of the unit filled in the awkward silence for several heartbeats.

'You're right. Pull up a chair, Athena, and tell me what you think we should be doing.'

She rolled her own chair over and plopped herself down, crossing her arms. 'I know it's important to be thorough. But it seems you're determined that this not be a random holdup by a stranger. Yet we see those all the time, don't we?'

'And we've got a handful of them on our desks right now.' Frank gestured in frustration at the pile of manila folders on one corner of his desk. 'I hate constantly trying to reassure vics when they know as well as I do that we're probably not going to find their attackers. And in this case, the victim died. If it's random, there's likely not going to be any evidence. I've seen it happen before. What else can we do but grasp at straws that might turn out to be evidence?'

'Are you following the evidence?' she

said. 'Or are you trying to make it fit?'

'There's still a gaping hole in the Del Oso side of things. It bothers me.'

'In general is your gut telling you the Del Osos murdered LaRoche?'

'Honestly, I'm not sure that my gut is telling me anything different from what my head is telling me, that Julie got killed in a random crime of opportunity. But my heart is telling me not to give up just yet.'

'Okay then. Let's go talk to Daniel again. But then maybe we need to start considering another avenue.'

'And just what do you suggest?'

'You said if it's random, there's likely not to be any salient evidence. Maybe there is, but it's not where you've looked. Maybe we need to start expanding and innovating. Looking in new ways.'

Her phone began to buzz in her pocket. She pulled it out, looked at the number and answered. 'This is Pardo.' Less than a minute later, she ended the call and re-pocketed the phone. 'This ought to be interesting. That was Cecilia Bedrosian. She wants to meet with me right now in the park.' After a moment she added, 'I guess I mean us.'

'No, you were right the first time. You've established some kind of trust with her. You go take it. I'll go pay that call on Daniel. Give me a buzz and let me know what transpires.'

Athena nodded and stood up.

'Hey, Athena.'

She had turned partway around and looked back at him.

'Be patient with me. Rome wasn't built in a day.'

She laughed.

'First time I think I ever saw you laugh. When we're back, you can start telling me your ideas about looking in new ways. And from now on, no elephants in the room, okay?'

'You got it, partner.'

As she walked away, Frank thought: was he ever going to get used to that word again?

★   ★   ★

Frank made a point of walking directly up to Daniel, who was giving instructions to a stock clerk. When he finished and the clerk bustled off, he looked expectantly at Frank.

'Is your father in the office, Daniel?'

'Actually, he's out back talking to a supplier. What's up?'

'I'm afraid I'm taking him in.'

'You're arresting him? Are you crazy?'

'I'm not exactly arresting him, just bringing him in for questioning. He's what we would call a person of interest in this case.'

'Aw, come on! What's the matter with you? You gotta know he had nothing to do with that fool's death! He was here all that night! Why are you harassing him like this? You're gonna kill the store as surely as all this other stuff will!'

'There's this nagging problem, Daniel. He was here, but you weren't.'

'I already told you where I was!'

'And we both know that's total nonsense.' The two men glared at each other. It began to draw the attention of customers further down the aisles. That made Daniel nervous.

'Okay, come on up to the office. I'll tell

you where I really was.'

In the cramped little office, Frank couldn't help noticing that the fish smell had still not abated, despite the obvious use of some kind of floral deodorizer. Now it just smelled like sweet flowery fish. Daniel closed the door behind him and leaned against a wall. Frank stood and waited.

'It was my brother.'

'Jesse? He came back to town?'

'I asked him to. We met at a bar over by the waterfront.'

'Go on.'

Daniel braced one arm over the other across his chest, looking defiant. 'My pop had nothing to do with this. It was all my idea.'

'What was all your idea?'

'Getting rid of LaRoche.'

★ ★ ★

Sunset Park was its formal name, but nobody in the city ever called it that. It was simply the Park, a four-block respite from urban sprawl, with rolling hills and wooden benches. The day was cool and overcast, with rain in the air, so there were very few people on the walkways or benches. Athena found the bench they had agreed upon, nestled as if under the protection of several high flowering bushes, and sat to wait. Soon she saw the familiar figure of Cecilia Bedrosian approaching, head down, hands in the pockets of her leather jacket. She sat down next to Athena without looking up or offering any kind of greeting. They both stared around the park, at the gray clouds in the sky, anywhere but at each other. Finally Cecilia broke the silence.

'My dad thinks I'm running some errands, so I haven't got very long.'

'So why are we here, Cecilia?'

The girl bit her lip and took a deep breath. 'It was all my fault.'

'You told me that the other day. You didn't lock the door all the way.'

'I think I know who one of the robbers was.'

'You said you didn't know them, that you were in the back and didn't see them.'

147

'But I still think I know.'

'Okay. Who is he?'

'His name is Tommy. He's kind of a boyfriend. I should say *was*. I haven't heard from him since then and I don't want anything to do with him.'

'Maybe you better back up a little bit here. How did this start?'

'I was seeing him on the sly. My dad is so old-fashioned . . . he doesn't want me hanging out with certain kinds of people. He wants me to spend all my time at the store and in the house.'

'And you had other ideas.'

Cecilia nodded. 'I know he needs my help, it's just him and me. But I want a life too.'

'So you met this Tommy, and you've been sneaking out to be with him?'

'Yeah. I thought he liked me and cared about me. He just seemed so cool, a little dangerous.'

It was Athena's turn to nod. 'The bad-boy thing.'

'I guess. But at the same time he was so sweet. I guess I was flattered that he liked me and paid so much attention to me.

Most handsome guys talk about themselves a lot. The conversation always seemed to center on me.'

'The way you're talking, you're not seeing him anymore.'

Cecilia shook her head violently. 'No. No, I'm not.'

'You think that Tommy robbed the café?'

'When I was hiding in the kitchen, I could hear his voice. It was muffled under the hood or whatever he was wearing. But I could tell. And I remembered he'd been asking all those questions, and I realized I'd told him all about the restaurant and when everybody left and when we closed and all that.'

'How about the second man? Do you know who he was?'

'No. His voice wasn't familiar. The second guy was the one who hurt my dad. He sounded pretty scary.'

'This Tommy — what's his last name?'

'He told me Karras. Now I'm not sure he ever told me the truth, what his real name might be.'

'You told me before that you didn't see

anybody, that there was nobody on the street when you went to lock up.'

'There wasn't. I didn't see anybody until they came into the café.'

Athena thought for a moment. The damp air was heavy and still. 'So you were afraid to say anything about this until now?'

Cecilia nodded. 'My father would kill me if he knew I was sneaking out to see him. And that other detective?'

'Detective Vandegraf.'

'Yeah. I'm sure he's a good guy and all, but . . . he just reminds me of my dad — very old-fashioned, you know?'

Athena smiled despite herself. 'He can be. But he's a very good man.'

'But I knew I couldn't tell him this. You just struck me as, I don't know, nicer, more understanding? Younger?'

'Whatever the reason, it's good that you're coming forward now. Have you seen or talked to Tommy since the robbery?'

'No. That's when I stopped seeing him. And I haven't heard from him since then. I think he was just playing me. Just a stupid little girl. He's probably laughing about me now.'

'If you had to, could you get in touch with him? Do you know where to find him?'

Cecilia shrugged. 'Maybe the place I used to meet him, where he hung out.'

'Did you ever meet any of Tommy's friends before this?'

'One or two, just really briefly, like they'd be with him when he came to meet me and they'd leave. I couldn't tell you anything about them.' Cecilia heaved a huge sigh and sunk her head between her shoulders. 'I don't believe what I've done.'

'So you're pretty sure that the guys you met, none of them were this second robber, then? And the first robber was definitely Tommy?'

'I'm pretty sure, yeah.'

'You're doing the right thing, Cecy. Can I call you that?'

'Sure. Everybody calls me that. Am I in a lot more trouble now?'

'Not if you're telling me the whole truth.'

'I am. This time I am.'

'Maybe we can find these guys and make this whole thing a little better.'

Something bothered Athena: Cecy still could not look at her while they talked.

★ ★ ★

'So you're telling me,' Frank asked Daniel, 'that you and Jesse got rid of Julie LaRoche?'

'No. Jesse wanted no part of it. He didn't even want to come back here. He only did it because I insisted pretty strongly. He heard me out and told me no.'

'What exactly did you tell him you wanted him to do?'

'Jesse's what our pop calls the *oveja negra*, the black sheep of the family. He's kind of infamous, almost a legend. I wouldn't have the slightest clue how to go about getting rid of someone. I figured he knew people.'

'So what happened?'

'He actually laughed at me. His innocent big brother. He said he'd never

152

killed anybody and he wasn't going to start. I told him he must have friends. He got real serious with me then, gave me this intense look. He said, 'I don't ever want to hear you say stupid stuff like that again, *hermano*.' Then he gave me a short lecture about the mistakes he had made in his own life. He didn't see himself as anybody to look up to, to emulate.'

'And then what?'

'Then we got kinda drunk together. We were there 'til pretty late. Finally he got up, said nobody was going to be seeing him for a long time, that it wasn't safe for him here anymore and he was gonna make a new life somewhere far away. He told me I couldn't tell anyone that he had come back to town. If I had to account for myself, I should just say I was with a dancer he knew named Candy. We hugged and he left. That was the last I saw of him.'

'How late did you leave there?'

'I don't know. I don't hold my liquor all that well. Maybe eleven.'

'Anybody else in the bar that saw you two there?'

'Just the bartender. An older lady, like fifty.'

Frank winced. He was somewhat beyond that milestone himself. 'And where's this waterfront bar with the grande dame behind the bar? Do you remember the name?'

'I think it's the Ancient Mariner.'

Frank shook his head. 'Perfect.'

⋆　⋆　⋆

The bartender at the Ancient Mariner was named Lu Fanning. The 'older lady' was likable and reasonably attractive, with full auburn hair and a roguish gleam in her eyes. She didn't look all that old to Frank. She was in fact the proprietor, having purchased the joint after a notorious shooting had occurred and her longtime employer had decided it was an opportune moment to return to his native New Orleans. She never liked his choice of ambience and had renovated and renamed the place in hopes of attracting a larger clientele. It apparently hadn't worked, but she seemed stoic about it.

Frank sipped a glass of club soda and politely bantered with her before getting to the point. 'Do you happen to remember your customers from last Wednesday night?'

'There we go. And here I hoped you'd come here because you'd heard of my vaunted charms, Detective. I remember almost every night here. One's not all that different from the next.'

'Do you recall two guys who might have come in here that night?'

'Sure. Two big tall Cuban guys.'

'How'd you know they were Cuban?'

'They were speaking in Cuban Spanish. I've spent some time in the Caribbean.'

'Could you hear what they were saying?'

'In general, no. First commandment of bartending, mind thy own business. But I caught a few words and when they ordered, I caught the accents. They were nice enough guys, looked like they might be related. One had kind of a rough exterior, scars and all that. The other guy seemed pretty young and sweet.'

'Sounds like they made an impression on you.'

Lu rolled her eyes. 'When they're your only customers, they tend to do that.'

'How late would you say they were here?'

'Maybe close to midnight. They put quite a few back. The tough one was drinking rum and Coke. The younger one drank beer.'

'Actually, if they're the guys I think, he's the older one.'

'Maybe in years. Not in life.'

'What was the tenor of their conversation like?'

'Listen to you, the 'tenor'! We don't get many men of letters here in this establishment! You mean like the drift?'

Frank slapped his hand on the back of his neck and sighed. 'Yes, like the drift.'

'They started out real hushed and serious, a little *contentious* almost. After a while the subject changed, they relaxed, and they just seemed to be shooting the bull, you know? You might say it began more *somber* and became more *congenial* with the passage of time.'

'Well, fancy that, a woman of letters in the establishment as well. What are the odds?'

'You just never know, Detective. Anything else I can help you with?'

'I think we're good.' Frank reached into his pocket and pulled out a couple of bills to leave on the counter.

'Your seltzer's on the house. Always happy to assist the city's finest.'

'And that's appreciated, madam, but I insist.' He left the bills and stood up from the stool.

She beamed a smile at him. 'Come on back when you're off duty. Maybe I'll start karaoke on Friday nights.'

Frank's phone began to buzz in his pocket. 'Not a big karaoke fan. I tend to shatter the glasses. Excuse me.'

The waterfront street wasn't exactly busy. He flipped open his phone as he walked the thirty or so steps from the bar to his car. 'What's up, Athena?'

'Frank, I think we might have a break in the Bedrosian robbery. Are you coming back to the unit soon, or can we meet up somewhere?'

'Heading back right now, in fact. See you there.'

★ ★ ★

'I'm hoping this Tommy Karras figures Cecy's too scared to say anything and that he'll still be hanging around.' They were sitting in the unit conference room, serious expressions over weathered mugs of hot coffee. Frank nodded as he absorbed her story.

'If we can pick him up, maybe he'll give up his pal.'

'This likely isn't his first job. Maybe we can make him for some other holdups.'

'Let's find the guy first. We can't even be totally sure he's good for the café yet.'

'There's still something that bothers me about that girl. Her story isn't quite right.'

'So far you've done great by giving her free rein. If there's more to her story, it may come out in time. Let's concentrate on this Karras character.' He raised his eyebrows. 'So she's sending us to a *bowling alley*? Really? She met him bowling?'

'She says she meets him at a dance club. He would seem to have some serious moves, according to her.'

'And not just on the dance floor, it would seem. So how does the bowling alley fit in?'

'He works there, or so she thinks. She would meet him there now and then, when she got off work and could sneak away. He didn't talk about himself all that much either. She wasn't all that clear on her Prince Charming. He's a mystery man. She isn't even sure at this point that he gave her his real name.'

'Lovely. What do girls see in a guy like this?'

'I'm not the person you should be asking.' Athena smiled. 'I was a good girl growing up. Hey, don't smirk. I was.'

'Oh, I believe it. You're still a straight arrow.'

'But I was definitely more aware than a lot of kids. Cecilia's very sheltered. Her father's pretty old-fashioned. I think this Tommy was sort of forbidden fruit. But besides that, from what she tells me, he showed a lot of interest in her. He didn't talk about himself, he talked about her. She must have found that very flattering.'

'So I assume this guy is astoundingly

handsome, awesomely captivating, and swept her off her feet. A regular Cary Grant. In a bowling alley.'

Athena shrugged. 'She's a kid. She told me he's very handsome and described him. Maybe we can find him over at the lanes.'

'I guess our plan is set then. Shall we?' Frank rose from his seat and downed the last of his coffee.

'And by the way, before you ask, yes, I do know who Cary Grant was. I'm not that young.'

'You know, Pardo, you've only been on the job here a couple of days and you're already getting snarkier. I think that's a good sign that you're loosening up. I must be rubbing off on you.'

'I didn't know any old guys knew what 'snarky' meant,' she stage-whispered as she followed him out of the conference room. Frank actually laughed.

★ ★ ★

The Gold Dust Bowl was situated in the basement of a building that also housed a pool hall and a rundown gym. The bowling alley had seen better days and had a kind of burnished patina to it — at least, Frank decided, that was how they would have spun it. The walls and floors were dark brown and orange, as much from tobacco and grime as from any kind of paint or wood varnish. There were twelve lanes and eight were occupied with bowlers. It struck him as the kind of place where street guys hung out, maybe some lower-echelon crime figures. Despite being in need of a facelift, the alley looked popular. It was a good under-the-radar kind of gathering joint.

After they both did a quick scan of the lanes, Frank stood by the door and let Athena walk to the counter and ask for Tommy. She had swapped her blazer for a stylish leather jacket from her car and looked somewhat less like a cop than he did. Maybe she wouldn't spook him. There was a short conversation, then the woman behind the counter disappeared through a door and an older man came out. He exchanged more words with Athena and pointed to his left to the end of the lanes. They both nodded, and she walked back to the doorway and Frank.

'His name's Tommy but it's not Karras. It's Lukacz. He works over in the bar.'

'Better get over there. That guy's going to tell him that a lady's asking for him. Maybe he'll be interested.'

Tommy Lukacz was clearing a small table when she walked in. She recognized him immediately: he looked to be in his late twenties, lean with long black hair. He watched her approach, placing some glasses on a round tray, then standing up straight, smiling at her as if trying to figure out who she might be.

'You're Tommy, right?' she said with a smile.

He hesitated and then said, 'Yeah. And you are . . . ?'

'Detective Pardo. I'm here to ask you a few questions.'

The attitude abruptly changed. 'Detective? I don't understand. Look, I'm really busy right now, and I can get in trouble if I stop to talk, you know? So . . . ' He was already turning to head for the door, leaving the tray of glasses on the table.

There was a larger, older man filling the narrow doorway. Tommy stopped, impatiently, to let him in so he could get by him. But Frank Vandegraf wasn't in any hurry to get out of the way.

'Stick around,' Frank said with a smile.

7

'I'm still not sure how you think I can help you,' the young man was saying as he sat in the interview room, idly rotating his can of soda in both hands. 'As I said, I don't know anything about the holdup in the café.' He stared at Frank and Athena across the scratched paint of the aging table.

'And you never got to talk to Cecilia about it because you stopped talking to her right after it happened,' Frank said.

'Uh, yeah. That's right.'

'You two had been seeing a lot of each other up until then, hadn't you?' Athena said. They watched as Tommy's head swiveled back and forth, looking at one and then the other.

'I wouldn't say a lot. We'd get together now and then.'

'So why did you stop? Why then?'

Tommy shrugged. 'No reason. I guess she lost interest in me.'

'It doesn't sound as if you were all that interested in her either.'

For some reason Frank found himself irritated by his smug smile and attitude. 'She's a very sweet kid. Kinda young and sheltered.'

'You did seem pretty interested in her for a while, though,' Frank said, leaning forward. 'Even if she was young and sheltered, as you put it. What happened to change your mind exactly?'

Tommy hesitated. 'Nothing. Nothing at all. It was never that big a deal. What, did she tell you something different?'

'We're more interested in what you tell us, Tommy,' said Athena. 'You have to see it from our viewpoint. You used to meet her all the time, go dancing, go to the movies, things like that. And all of a sudden, her father's restaurant gets robbed and now you won't have anything to do with her. You see how that looks to us?'

'Wait a minute, are you saying you think I had something to do with that? Am I a, whattaya call it, a suspect here?'

Frank raised his hands and smiled

slightly. 'Let's not get ahead of ourselves here, Tommy. We're not accusing you of anything here, we're just asking you for your help. You're what we would call a person of interest.'

'A person of interest. You mean like someone who knows stuff they can tell you?'

'Yes, sort of. You haven't been arrested or anything. We appreciate you came with us voluntarily and want to help us out.' Tommy nodded. It wasn't clear to Frank how many lights were on behind his eyes and how much he actually understood of what was going on here.

'It did kind of surprise me when you tried to get away from me in the bowling alley, though,' Athena added. 'Like you had something to hide. You don't have anything to hide though, right?'

'Oh no, right, nothing. I wasn't trying to get away. I was just a little confused, was all. I sometimes get in trouble at work because stuff hasn't gotten done, or they find me talking to someone, you know?'

'So tell us a little more about your relationship with Cecilia. How long ago did you meet her?'

'Let's see. She was with friends at a dance club. Insanity.'

'What was insane about it?' asked Frank.

'No, I mean that's the name of the club. Insanity.'

'Ah. Okay. And when was this?'

'Maybe a couple months ago, like that.'

'And how did you two meet?'

'One of her friends knew one of my friends and we were all introduced. I danced with her and then we arranged to meet up again after that night.'

'So, what, you would go pick her up and take her out?'

'Uh-uh. She said her old man was pretty strict. She kinda had to sneak out to see me. She'd call me and tell me she could get out and we'd meet at the Gold Dust. A couple times I met her over at the Cineplex and we'd see a movie.'

'It all sounds awfully clandestine,' said Frank. 'So you didn't consort much in public.'

'Consort? Naw. We went dancing a couple times. Went out to eat now and then. Mostly just hung out. Sometimes she'd come by while I was working. I had to pretend I wasn't.'

Sterling employee, Frank mused. What a catch this guy would be for any fair young damsel. 'Did Cecilia tell you much about herself, her family?'

'She told me a few things. I know her old man kept her on a tight leash and that she was pretty bored with working at the restaurant. I guess he's pretty old school.'

'What did you tell her about yourself?' asked Athena, watching him carefully.

'The usual stuff. She seemed more interested in talking about herself.'

'Did you tell her your real name?'

Tommy hesitated. 'What do you mean?'

'I mean, didn't you tell her your name was Karras? It seems your name is Lukacz, isn't it?'

It began to dawn on the young man that they knew more than they had been letting on. 'Uh, yeah,' he drawled slowly. 'I figured, she looked Greek, so she might feel more comfortable hanging out with me if she thought I was, too . . . '

Both detectives exhaled audibly. Frank

ran a hand over his thinning forehead. He tried to imagine a perspective from which this dumb hunk of meat would seem charming and captivating, as Cecilia had apparently found him to be.

'Actually,' interjected Athena, 'she's not Greek. But I happen to be half Greek, and you don't seem Greek to me whatsoever.'

'Uh,' grunted Tommy, a perplexed expression on his face. 'Well, whatever.'

'Just curious, does that ever work? When you tell a girl you're a Greek named Karras, I mean. Or whatever names you try with them?'

The perplexed expression turned to a dumb grin, a feeble attempt at cute. It got no reaction, so he just shrugged.

'You said you weren't all that interested in her, but you seem to have gone to some trouble to try to make a good impression.'

'It was just a thing, you know?'

'No,' Athena said, folding her arms, scowling. 'I don't know. What is that supposed to mean?'

'Supposing we told you,' said Frank,

'that someone saw you the afternoon of the robbery and was able to identify you in the café?'

'What? Wait a minute!' Tommy looked back and forth at the two stone-faced detectives, who just stared back at him.

'We might just have enough, in fact, to promote you from person of interest to suspect, Tommy. What do you think about that?'

'There's no way!'

'So help us out,' said Athena. 'The holdup took place two weeks ago today, around three o'clock. Can you tell us where you were then? All you have to do is show us you were somewhere else, where people saw you, and you're off the hook.'

'I must have been at work! I was working, like I do most Tuesdays!'

'So if we go talk to the manager or the owner, they'll tell us you were there all afternoon, right?'

Tommy Lukacz hesitated. 'I'd, uh, rather you didn't do that. Um . . . I'm in a lot of hot water at work now as it is.'

'What I'm hearing,' said Frank, 'is that

nobody's going to be able to vouch for your whereabouts two weeks ago. Am I right?'

'I think I want to go now. I don't want to talk to you anymore.'

'Oh, come on, Tommy. Do I need to read you your rights and place you under arrest?' Frank made a large production of pushing back the metal chair with a loud rasp across the ground, and lifting himself to an upright position. Glaring down at Tommy, he suddenly looked awfully big and very annoyed.

The last of the young man's fading bravado dissolved. All at once, he looked like a frightened kid. 'Wait,' he said. 'It wasn't my fault. The way things went. It wasn't my fault.'

Frank sat back down and waited. It took a long time and a fair amount of effort to keep Tommy Lukacz on track. The expression 'herding cats' occurred to Frank as he and Athena struggled to keep the scatterbrained suspect on point.

'But it wasn't me, it was him, the other guy.'

'The other guy. You keep saying the

other guy,' said Athena. 'Who is this other guy?'

'Bruno. The other guy.'

'So who's this Bruno, and how do you know him?'

'He's one of the guys that comes by the alley all the time. There's a lot of players hanging out there.'

'By players,' Frank said, 'you mean wise-guy types?'

'Yeah, and wannabe wise guys, the kind of guys who are looking to get into the game, you know? If you know who to talk to, it can be like job interviews.'

'So this Bruno, is he a player, as you call them, or is he a wannabe?'

'He strikes me as a pretty serious dude. He's not major league yet, but he's done some stuff, if you know what I mean?'

'And you were interested in doing some stuff with him?' Athena asked.

'Well, there's just not much going on for me right now, you know?'

Frank really wanted to ask him to stop the 'you knows' but they had finally gotten him on something resembling a linear track and he didn't want to derail it, so he said nothing.

'I had a few conversations with him, just small talk, and I was kinda impressed. He seemed to know his way around. I thought he would be a good person to know.'

'So, what, you two decided to pull a job together?'

Tommy rested his head in his hand. 'I guess I was trying to impress him and I started talking big. Next thing I know he says to me, 'Are you gonna put your money where your mouth is?' and I felt like I had to come up with something. All I could think of was the café where this girl had been telling me she worked. Bruno seemed interested at that. He told me I should, whattaya call it, cultivate her, ask her a lot of questions, find out about the place. So I did. I started asking to see her and got her to talk about herself and her family and the restaurant. She said there were days when her father left the money in the register for a few days before banking it. And she said that at the end of the day, there was just her and her father. Bruno said that's when we

173

should hit the place.' He looked up back and forth at the two detectives. 'It was just supposed to be walk in, show the guns, scare them, take the money. Nobody would recognize us, nobody would get hurt.'

'But it didn't go that way,' said Frank.

'This guy . . . I had no idea. He's a crazy dude. Scary-crazy. We got to the register and pulled out these bags and filled them with the money and I figured that was it. But he wasn't happy with how much was in the register. He started yelling there must be more. Then he just started hitting the old man. I mean, like beating on the guy. He was really angry. I was afraid he was going to kill him. Then he yelled at me to get out of there fast, so we ran out.'

'How did you get to the café?'

'We drove and parked around the corner. We pulled on the masks as we walked to the café. When we left, we just kept them on until we got to the car. I don't think anybody saw us. Bruno said even if somebody did, odds were they wouldn't want to get involved.'

'Whose car was it?'

'Bruno swiped it, I'm pretty sure. Then he wiped it and left it somewhere.'

'Where'd you go after the robbery?'

'Some empty garage or something that belongs to a friend of his. We split up the money in the two bags. He was still ticked off that it wasn't anywhere near what I had said it was gonna be. He told me to find my way home from there and he took off.'

'You didn't try to go hide or anything? You weren't worried that Cecilia might have recognized you or that somebody saw you?'

Tommy got lost in what passed for thought. 'Bruno said I had nothing to worry about. I should just act normal, show up for work as usual, not do anything different. She wouldn't tell anyone, nobody was going to say anything. They were too scared to look carefully at us and we had the masks.'

'How about the guns?' asked Frank. 'Where'd they come from?'

'Bruno brought them. I don't know guns. Couldn't tell you what they were. They were revolvers, I guess meant to look big and scary. He brought the ski masks, even gave me a pair of gloves so we wouldn't leave prints on anything.'

'Quite a teacher, huh?' asked Frank.

'This guy Bruno,' said Athena. 'What's his real name?'

Tommy shrugged. 'I dunno. Everybody calls him Bruno. Not many people use their real names that hang around at the alley, you know?'

'Including you, right?'

'Well, I work there, so they know my name.'

'So what does Bruno look like?'

'Big guy. I'd say over six feet. Shaves his head. Keeps his beard stubbly.'

'What color are his eyes, do you know?'

'Man, he's got scary eyes. Wolf eyes. Like clear marbles.'

'But what color would you say?'

'Kinda gray, I guess.'

'Has he been back to the alleys since the robbery?'

Tommy shook his head. 'Haven't seen him.'

'Do you have a way to get in touch with him?'

Tommy shook his head again. 'We

always just met at the alleys.'

'What about the money?'

'It was only around six or seven hundred for each of us. I kinda spent it.'

'And you've been avoiding Cecilia since then, right?'

'I didn't want her involved in this. I felt terrible about what happened to her old man. I figured I should stay away from her. If she came looking for me I'd tell her to get lost. But she never came back. That's a good thing, right?'

The two detectives sat with stony glares. He looked back and forth at them, getting no reaction from either.

'I've never done anything like this before. I swear. And she had nothing to do with it either. It was Bruno, the other guy. You gotta believe me. I've never been in trouble like this before.'

'Help us find this guy Bruno,' Frank said evenly, 'and you'll help yourself as well.'

By the time the interview was over, they had convinced Tommy to make a written statement and contacted the prosecutor's office to send over an assistant DA to negotiate a plea deal. They both felt exhausted. Guys like Tommy Lukacz just did that to you.

They plotted their next move in the elevator back to their unit.

'If we can find this Bruno character,' Frank said, 'we might have a good case with Tommy turning on him. The trick is to find him.'

Athena nodded. 'What if I reach out to some of the uniforms I know? He doesn't sound familiar to me, but maybe our gray-eyed perp is known on the street somewhere.'

'Why not? Nothing to lose.'

'There are still things that bother me about Cecilia. It's a remarkable coincidence that those guys showed up the very night she forgot to lock the door. Something's missing from the story.'

Frank nodded. 'I think you're going to do okay here. You strike me as someone who won't let go of something until you're sure you've got everything in place.'

'Sort of like you. You're still not willing to accept Julie LaRoche's death was a random act, are you?'

'Nope. In fact I think I'm going to make a few more calls as soon as I'm back at my desk.'

* * *

She picked up in the same don't-waste-my-time way. 'This is Lorena Park.'

'Ms. Park, Detective Vandegraf here. I assume you remember me from our last conversation?'

'Of course, Detective. Are you the one that's obstructing my story?'

'Obstructing your story? What are you talking about?'

'The Bodega Building, as you called it. Why is there an effort to scare me off?'

Frank took a deep breath. 'I've got nothing to do with that. Someone contacted you about your story? Who was it?'

'Someone who identified themselves as a Special Agent with the FBI. Aren't they all special though? Well, it might make my job harder, but it's not going to stop me. They even expected me to turn over my notes. That is not going to happen.'

'Ms. Park, you might not believe me, but we're on the same side here. I've been frozen out of that area as well. In fact I was hoping you might be my only resource right now.'

'What's so important about that building anyway? Apparently my instincts were pretty good about Bizel Financial.'

'What else do you know about it?'

'First one to give up what they know loses, Detective. So what do you know?'

'Nothing that you don't. Guaranteed. My only interest is how Julius LaRoche fit into this.'

'I can't help you much there. I've found nothing to indicate that he was anything other than the buyer they lined up. He was unprincipled enough to jump at the chance and not ask questions.'

'The other tenants — besides the market and the restaurant. They seem to have cleared them out. They didn't renew leases and didn't bring in new tenants.'

'Makes the building easy to turn over for a profit,' said Park. 'That's all any of these people cared about. Hang the tenants.'

'You don't see anything in this that could have gotten Julie killed?'

'Bizel itself seems to be trying to stay pretty clean of mob tactics. They're a white-collar crime outfit. I'm not saying it's totally out of the question, but it's incongruous for them to kill someone in such an obvious way.'

'For an investigative reporter, you seem to be pretty reticent, Ms. Park.'

'Detective, in some ways your job and mine are similar. We can't get caught up in what we'd like to have happened. We have to follow the hard evidence. As much as I'd love a juicy murder conspiracy, I just don't see it.'

★ ★ ★

Frank opened the folder and pulled out the newspaper clippings. He re-read Lorena Park's impassioned article on the Webleyview evictions and stared at the photographs. The *Sentinel's* article pulled no punches in setting up Julie LaRoche as the classic villain who threw indigents, children and oldsters into the streets. All that was missing was a picture of Julie twirling a long handlebar mustache as he cackled. There were photos of several of the people who had been displaced, including Lorena Park's relatives. The article even included a photo of the gravestone of the evicted woman who had died, Camilla Wardell Valdespino. Her full name and birth and death dates were prominently engraved onto the stone. She had been sixty-one when she died. He peered intently at the photos and the article, re-reading it over and over. There was something . . .

'Hey! Frank! Frank!'

He looked up. Athena was hanging up her desk phone, staring at him across the space between their desks.

'I've put the word out on this Bruno guy. Let's see what comes back.'

'Good.' He stared back down at the clippings. 'There's something else here. How many bus routes do you think there are along Institution Boulevard?'

'Not many. Three, maybe. Why, what do you have in mind?'

Leon Simpkins happened to be walking

by and found himself in the crosstalk between Frank and Athena. 'Whoa. Excuse me for interrupting.'

'No problem, Detective Simpkins.'

'Call me Leon. And you're Athena, right? How do you like the unit so far? Is this guy doing right by you?'

'Interesting place,' Athena replied. 'And Frank's great.'

'Give him time.' Simpkins grinned.

'Hey, Leon,' Frank said, 'do you happen to know the Gold Dust Bowl, in the basement under the Pool Cue and some kind of gym?'

'Do I know it? Unfortunately, yeah. Art and I have spent a little time down there. A lot of dumbbells.' That was his pet term for the lazier, less clever locals who nonetheless aspired to become under-world kingpins. They were often gym rats or pool hustlers.

'Any chance you'd know anything about a guy called Bruno? Big guy, shaved head, stubbly beard?'

'That could be a handful of guys.'

'He's supposed to have these gray piercing eyes, kind of scary, like a wolf.'

'Now that sounds like . . . what's his name?' He turned to call to his partner across the room. 'Hey, Art! C'mere, wouldya?'

Art Dowdy threaded his way between desks and around other personnel, the usual doleful scowl on his face.

'Athena, you remember the Mortician,' Frank said. Dowdy nodded to Athena and she nodded back.

'I'd prefer you called me Art,' he said seriously.

'Art, do you remember that big guy with the gray eyes we questioned a few weeks back over at the Pool Cue?' asked Simpkins.

'Bronstein,' Dowdy said. 'No. Bromberg. That guy?'

'That's the one! Bromberg! You remember his first name?'

'How could I forget it? Hildebrandt!'

'What?' asked Frank. 'You're kidding me!'

'That's right,' smiled Simpkins. 'That was his name.'

'Ever hear him called Bruno?' asked Frank.

'We heard him called a lot of names,

mostly behind his back. A lot of guys avoid him. Mean SOB. He kinda scares them.'

'So what did you have him for?'

'There were a couple of robberies nearby, and we developed a theory that whoever was pulling the jobs might be basing their operations there. Like I said, lots of would-be tough guys hang out in the pool hall or the bowling alley. Bromberg was one of the guys who looked good to us.'

Dowdy looked even more downcast. 'Couldn't find enough to bring anybody in. But we still liked him for a couple of those jobs.'

'What kind of jobs?'

'A tavern a few blocks away, a liquor store. Both similar MOs. They came in late at night, faces masked, flashing big guns that looked more for fright, seemed to know the places and their routines, got the proprietor to open the register. In both cases there was only one person in the place, and both of them got knocked around before the perps left.'

'Two-man jobs, both of them?'

'That's right.'

'Why'd you like this Bromberg for them?'

'Of all the guys hanging out there, he best fit the description of the bigger guy.'

Frank and Athena exchanged glances. 'Any idea how we might find him?'

'He gave us an address,' said Simpkins. 'Maybe he's stupid enough to actually be there.'

As luck would have it, he was. Two uniforms brought him in without a fight.

* * *

'You're serious?' Bromberg was sitting at the interview table across from Athena and Frank, leaning back in his chair, stretching out his long legs, a cocky smile on his face. 'Again with the holdups? You guys keep bringing me in about these holdups. Can't you find the real bad guys, you gotta keep bothering me?'

'We've got your buddy Tommy,' said Frank calmly, scratching the side of his nose. 'He's got the fear of God in him, let me tell you.'

Bromberg snorted. 'The little wimp. He's no buddy of mine. He's got a great imagination, that one. Wants to be a hot-shot gangster.' He cast a narrow-eyed gaze back and forth at them. 'The little rat is talking? I'm not saying I did anything, mind you. But he's saying I did?'

'Maybe you'd better tell us your side of the story,' Athena said, 'seeing how he's telling us his. And you don't seem to come off too well in his version.'

'We've also got a witness who got a very good look at those unusual eyes of yours, even with the ski mask,' added Frank.

Clearly Bromberg's confidence suddenly took a small bump. He had figured that Tommy was too scared to say anything to anyone; that the Bedrosians were too scared and confused to step up to make an identification. Guys like this, thought Frank, were convinced they had everybody frightened. They figured they could carry on their lives with impunity. They didn't have to hide or keep a low profile. Up until now he had been right.

'Maybe I should ask for my lawyer,'

Bromberg said, sitting up.

'Sure,' said Frank. They both stood up. 'He or she will very likely advise you to cop a plea in exchange for giving up the rest of your buddies.'

'The rest of my buddies? What's that supposed to mean?'

'Oh, we're not done with you, Bruno. There are two other detectives out there who are very frustrated about some other similar robberies. There are going to be enough charges to keep you locked up for a long, long time. Unless you start thinking about a deal.'

They read him his rights and handcuffed him, then knocked on the door for an officer to take him to a holding cell.

'Do you think the Bedrosians will come in and ID him?' asked Frank as they waited at the elevator.

Athena nodded. 'I think so. Mr. Bedrosian for sure. I'm interested in how Cecilia is going to react to all of this.'

'Good work on this one. You're off to a good start.'

Athena, trying to maintain a professional demeanor, was clearly pleased and couldn't resist a smile. 'Thanks. Now what about the LaRoche case? You said you got something new?'

'I think so. If I'm right, we just need to do a little bit of homework. Are you up for that?'

'Of course. What are we doing?'

'Bus schedules,' said Frank.

8

'I appreciate your coming in like this to help us, Mr. Wardell,' Frank said cheerily as he opened the door to the interview room and gestured for him to enter.

'I'm only too happy to help, Detective, but I really don't know how I can. There's nothing I haven't told you already.'

Athena was adjusting a video monitor and placing a remote control on the table. She turned and extended her hand with a smile.

'You may remember Detective Pardo,' said Frank.

'No, I can't say as we've met, have we?' said Wardell, mystified, taking her hand.

'Sure we have,' she said. 'I was in uniform last time.'

'Ah . . . yeah . . . you were the patrolman . . . I mean, patrolwoman . . . patrol person . . . ?'

'Patrol officer, right. Thanks for helping us out here. Have a seat. Sorry the room's not all that comfortable.'

Wardell looked around the room as Frank closed the door. 'Didn't you say you wanted me to try to ID somebody for you? Where are they?'

'Actually, they're on the video we're going to show you, okay?'

'Sure,' Wardell said, his mystified look deepening. He and Frank sat down. Athena remained standing, picked up the remote and aimed it at the monitor, bringing a video to life.

'It turns out the buses have security cameras,' said Frank. 'We were able to pull scenes from this one. Watch, now.'

'But there were no buses going by when the guy was killed,' Wardell said.

'Just watch, okay?'

The camera's angle was over the shoulder of the bus driver towards the front door. The video was slightly grainy and the color was washed out, but they could clearly see as the bus came to a halt, the door opened, and two people climbed aboard the bus. Athena froze the action.

'There,' said Frank. 'Do you see that

person still standing in the kiosk at the stop?'

'What about him?'

'Isn't that you, Mr. Wardell?'

'Uh . . . it could be, maybe. Hard to tell.'

'There's not much color in this footage but you can see that strong orange color of your jacket. That looks exactly like what you were wearing that night, doesn't it?'

'If you say so, sure. There were a couple of buses that went by while I was waiting.'

'Do you remember people at your stop, then, getting on that bus?'

'Yeah, now that you mention it. Sure.'

Athena started the action again. The bus door closed, leaving Wardell in the kiosk, and pulled away.

'You were still waiting for your bus at that point then.'

'Uh-huh.'

'The number ten, was that right?'

'Yes. The number ten was my bus. It doesn't come very often that time of the evening.' Wardell looked at them both expectantly. 'I'm confused. Why are you showing me this? Where's the person you want me to try to identify?'

'Mr. Wardell, we're confused too right now. Maybe you can help us out here. You see, that was the number ten bus.'

'It couldn't have been!' Wardell exclaimed.

'I suppose you didn't happen to notice the date and time register in the lower corner of the video. There. That was the number ten bus . . . it came by that stop at six fourteen p.m.'

Athena stopped the video again. 'A good forty-five minutes before you saw Mr. LaRoche killed and called it in, you were already at that bus stop. Why was that?'

'There must be some mistake,' Wardell stammered.

In the short awkward silence that followed, Frank opened a manila folder in front of him and extracted a large photo. He turned it so Wardell could see it. 'By the way, our condolences, Mr. Wardell, on the recent death of your mother. That is your mother's grave, isn't it?'

He looked numbly at the image. 'Yes. Yes it is. Thank you. What does that have to do with anything?'

'This is where we were hoping you could help us,' said Frank, leaning in towards the young man. 'An awful lot of people *could* have been suspected of killing Julius LaRoche. He was disliked, even hated, by many people because he did some pretty terrible things. One of those things was to evict a woman from her home, a woman who then slipped into indigence and died. By a strange coincidence, the only witness to that killing was the son of that woman. And stranger still, that witness had been standing at that very place for probably an hour or more.'

Frank and Athena now both leaned closer in to Wardell, who was looking at them with wide eyes. 'Come on. Once we figured out what we were looking for, we found . . . well, enough to hold you and to charge you.'

'You'd be amazed,' added Athena, 'the places there are security cameras that will place you on that corner for such a long time.'

'You were the one who fingered him,' Frank said. 'Maybe you wore that orange jacket so the killer would see you?'

'I'm guessing you phoned him to alert him,' Athena added. 'You had to wait a long time for your intended victim to come out.'

Frank looked at Athena. 'He probably cleared his phone history afterward, too. That'd be the smart thing.'

'But perhaps it didn't occur to him. We could get his phone records from the phone company,' Athena replied.

They both turned to Wardell.

'You wouldn't object if we checked your cell phone records, would you, Mr. Wardell?'

The young man stared, mouth partway open.

'Cameron,' said Frank earnestly, 'you're in this pretty deep. I don't see any way you're getting out of this.'

'And frankly,' added Athena, 'you're our only connection to the guy who pulled the trigger. And if we don't find him . . . well, there's just you, and you can imagine how that's going to go.'

Frank nodded thoughtfully. 'There's a lot of publicity on this case. And Athena and I are feeling the pressure from above, let me tell you. The DA really wants someone to go down for this. And right now, you're what we've got to give him.' He reached out and laid a hand on Wardell's shoulder. 'The best you can hope for is to make it easier for yourself and cooperate.'

Athena also leaned in closer to Wardell. 'Cameron, you know what I'm sensing here? You're not the kind of guy who contracts a murder. You know that and it's been eating away at you ever since you set it up, am I right? You're way out of your element. Part of you is terrified of this guy and his world — is he going to come back and take you out, just to be safe? You don't know, do you? The greater part of you, though, must be haunted with guilt.' Wardell looked up at her. 'Most people who commit this kind of crime, they're neither smart enough nor decent enough to care. Then we see people like you, who make terrible mistakes and are smart and decent enough at heart to recognize it. Take it from me, you're never going to be free of it until you come completely clean.'

It seemed to hit a nerve. Frank was impressed at Athena's tactic. Wardell kept staring at Athena, but there was something different in his eyes now.

It was a slow process. It took them another hour to get Cameron Wardell to piece together the improbable story.

Warren and Camilla Wardell had not been a good match for one another. By the time Cameron was a teenager, their fights had become increasingly bitter and their incompatibility clear. He was too young to comprehend many of the issues between them, and perhaps he had the tendency to see things in very black-and-white terms. In any case, he found himself siding with his father; and when the split finally came, he chose to leave with him. Camilla ultimately agreed. They moved out of state and had no communication with her thereafter. The divorce was accomplished long-distance through attorneys.

It took some years before Cameron began to see the dark side of his father, who began to drink heavily and relinquish his responsibilities, finding it harder to keep a job. They moved into a series of progressively seedier apartments. One day, on a drunken bender, Warren Wardell got into his car and never made it home. Cameron was twenty-three.

He had to grow up in a hurry. He scraped together what little resources were left and gave his father a cheap burial. Warren's legacy consisted of a stack of cardboard boxes and a small closet of old clothes. In the process of disposing of everything, Cameron read letters that his father had kept. It shed a new light on his parents' relationship.

There was no reason for him to stay, so he decided to leave that world behind him and return to the city of his childhood, to try to find his mother, reconnect with her . . . tell her he was sorry. He had no idea where to start, but he found a cheap apartment and a job in a restaurant that actually paid decently. He had always had an affinity for computers, so he found extension courses with the aim of a career in internet technology, possibly web design or development.

He discovered that Camilla Wardell had remarried and that her second marriage had not been any more successful than her first. No sooner had Paul Valdespino departed than she received the notice that her apartment building had been purchased and she was being evicted. Perhaps that was the final straw in her tenuous ability to cope with reality, but acquaintances of hers told Cameron that she had taken to wandering the streets and had one day been found dead. Her death had occurred only weeks before he had arrived to look for her.

Paul Valdespino had come forth to pay for a funeral service and a headstone. He wasn't hard to find. Cameron did not particularly like the man, but they had something in common: an overwhelming sense of guilt. They talked; and when they parted, Valdespino tucked an envelope into Cameron's pocket. It contained five thousand dollars in cash. Valdespino walked away and they had not spoken since.

Cameron found the newspaper articles about the Webleyview evictions and conversions. There was one name mentioned repeatedly of the man who was painted as the villain in the case: Julius LaRoche. He was so despicable that the writer of the article even referred to him repeatedly as La Roach.

Cameron had an envelope full of unreported money and a seething sense of frustration and guilt. He formed a plan of vengeance. It was totally deranged; but in his state of mind, it made sense. The villain — the cockroach — would pay.

'How did you find this guy?' asked Frank.

Wardell raised his eyebrows and made a gesture with his hands. 'The dark web,' he said. 'Of course.'

'What in hell is the dark web?' asked Frank.

'It's the inaccessible part of the internet,' Athena said. 'It's not indexed by search engines and such. The dark web's the site of a lot of illicit, untraceable activity.'

Frank looked baffled. 'If it's inaccessible, how do you get to it?'

'You have to know how,' said Wardell. 'You need special software, configurations, authorizations, stuff like that.'

Athena seemed to know what she was talking about here, which was good, since Frank felt even more like a dinosaur than usual.

'And how did you know how to navigate your way around it?' she asked.

'I learned about it from the people in my classes. Then it was just a matter of trial and error to find what I was looking for.'

'And you were looking for a professional killer?'

Wardell nodded. 'As I got deeper into the dark web, I started thinking maybe I should find someone a little less scary. There are international syndicate kinds of guys — expensive, serious. To be honest, they were terrifying. There were other sites with people advertising that they would administer beatings, put people in the hospital. I thought one of those might be safer to negotiate with. They were like . . . friendlier.'

'Friendlier,' repeated Frank, dumbfounded.

'How exactly does this work?' asked Athena. 'How do you contact the person?

How do you pay them? How can you be sure it's not a scam on their part?'

'The sites where they advertise link you to a private chat room where you can work it out. You pay in bitcoin and arrange the details.'

'Bitcoin?' asked Frank.

'It's a digital payment medium,' said Athena. 'And when you pay, it's gone, no trail. So you set up an online bank account?'

'Yeah, that's easy.'

' . . . and took a chance that this guy wasn't going to just take your money and run?'

Wardell shrugged. 'I took a chance. I gambled that someone advertising a lower level of crime might be less likely to rip me off.'

The detectives looked at one another. This was definitely a young guy way out of his comfort zone.

'I scouted around and found a guy who advertised various acts of violence. He'd show up and deliver a beating. He had different levels of harm and kind of a price list. He limited the area in which he worked to about a five-hundred-mile radius, and I was in it. For fifteen hundred dollars or so, he'd put someone in the hospital. I sent him an inquiry — would he be willing to go all the way, and for how much? He said sure. We agreed on a price of three thousand and set a date.'

Frank shook his head. What kind of brave new world was he living in? 'Did you meet with this guy?'

'No. That was an important point — we never saw each other. We made general arrangements and he gave me a number to call. I gave him the time and the place; told him to dress like a gang member and make it look like a mugging. I told him to be nearby, described what I'd be wearing, and said I'd give him a call when the target showed up.'

'You didn't expect to wait as long as you did.'

'No, but I figured that was an advantage, since the street kept getting emptier.'

'So you went shopping for a professional killer, with no idea what this guy looked like, or if he'd even show up,' said Athena. 'Pretty stupid. A lot of things could have happened to you, starting with him simply scamming you out of your money, and going downhill from there. The dark web is no place to be messing around.'

'I know, I know. But it was the only way I could figure to do it. I don't exactly hang around with criminals.'

The detectives exchanged a look. That was pretty clear. He looked totally over his head right now, and he seemed to be developing a severe twitch.

'What's his name?' asked Frank. He was repelled but fascinated by the sordid novelty of the whole tale.

'I only knew him by his screen name. Black Flag.'

'Well, he's got a flair for cheap dramatics. So you had a number to call him when you saw LaRoche. Probably a cheap burner that he got rid of right afterward, but we're going to look at it anyway. You told him to rob him, then kill him?'

'Yeah. I told him to take his money,

wallet, anything he had. He could keep any money or valuables, but he should get rid of anything incriminating. I told him to burn everything.' Wardell shuddered. 'I knew what was coming but I wasn't ready. When I heard the gun go off . . . it was like it wasn't real. It was awful.'

'And can we assume you haven't had any contact with Mr. Black Flag ever since?'

Wardell shook his head. 'Nope. Got no idea where he went or who he was. After that, I really didn't want to talk to him ever again.'

'Cameron, you realize this is the one card you've got to play? There's got to be some way you can contact this guy and bring him back here.'

'I don't know,' Wardell said. Suddenly the gravity of the situation seemed to be hitting home. He reminded Frank of a character he had seen in a Renaissance painting of the Last Judgment . . . a sinner being borne to hell.

Frank pondered for a minute. 'I assume he's still advertising on that site.'

'I guess so.'

'Would he be willing to come back and take out somebody else for you?'

'What do you mean?'

'What if you — or someone saying they were you — had another job for him?'

'Are you serious?'

'In a manner of speaking.'

Wardell didn't quite catch on. He stared, uncomprehending. Frank rubbed his neck and took a deep breath. 'That's how we bring this guy back.'

★ ★ ★

'I'm finding it hard to believe all of this,' Frank mused, the two of them again at his desk. 'A dark secret internet with drug dealing and killers for hire.'

'It gets much worse,' said Athena. 'Much worse. Sick stuff. It's a perilous place, a good place for most people to stay away from.'

'Sounds like it's got its share of idiots and fools as well.'

'None of this would have happened if the guy *had* just taken his bitcoin and never showed up.'

'If only,' sighed Frank. 'I guess we didn't luck out. Especially Julie.'

'There's one saving grace. The payment was totally untraceable and there was no evidence of the transaction. He would have gotten away with this if you hadn't made the connection.'

Frank nodded. 'Right now Wardell's pretty scared. We might still not have that strong a case against him and he might start figuring that out sooner or later. We have to hope this works.'

'Frank, I have a feeling. We're getting this guy.'

★   ★   ★

Cortado Lane was appropriately named. Its name was Spanish for 'cut off,' and it was indeed a short dead-end street, a forgotten area of mostly abandoned old houses and small brownstones, with outdated lighting fixtures that the city likely hoped it would never have to replace. What spare lighting did exist was blotted by thick overgrown trees. The figure standing in the deep shadow of an alleyway, watching a house across the street, decided this was very much to his liking.

He once again went over the email instructions he had memorized earlier: ADDRESS IS 9678 CORTADO. HE RETURNS HOME EVERY NIGHT AT NINE, LIKE CLOCKWORK. NO STREET LIGHTS IN FRONT OF THE HOUSE. STREET USUALLY VERY EMPTY.

He would wait for his subject to appear, cross the street and push him into the space between the buildings, and begin his work.

The message had been simple and not overly specific. DON'T KILL HIM.

The dark figure's real name was Edgar. He had no idea what the name of his intended victim was, and didn't care. He had a description of his objective and he was just happy that he had gotten another paying job. He was a little disappointed to not get another opportunity to make a kill; the last one had been particularly enjoyable, a step up. But in general he enjoyed his work. He decided he had finally found his calling: he liked to hurt people. The day he had been shown that hidden corner of the internet had been a turning point in his life. He never had to travel more than a few hours from his home and was making a nice living, tax free, untraceable.

He looked at his watch. Five minutes to nine. He heard footsteps up the dark sidewalk. A dark hunched-over figure, loud hard-soled shoes scraping on the pavement. He took a quick look up and down the street, satisfied that there were only the two of them. A true predator, Edgar snapped into total concentration mode. There was only him and his prey.

Edgar wore soft-soled athletic shoes that made no noise as he moved among the shadows and crossed the street. He fell in about ten steps behind the ambling figure, closing the gap between them. He timed it perfectly. He was within arm's length of the hunched-over man just as they reached the gap before the building. He reached out to grab the victim's shoulders, ready to shove him into the dark narrow abyss. He was so intently concentrating on his target that he failed to notice several other dark shapes emerging from nearby shadows of buildings and trees and converging upon him.

Suddenly the hunched-over man was noticeably taller. He had spun around and shoved the barrel of a police service automatic right into Edgar's face. Several pairs of hands grabbed him at once, and he found himself being wrestled easily to the ground.

'Well, what have we here?' asked Frank, holstering his weapon and peering down at the dark struggling figure being held to the pavement by three of his colleagues.

★   ★   ★

All of the unit's interview rooms were dingy, but the one they jokingly called the Fortress was the grimmest of the lot. Grayish-green paint was peeling off the walls and a couple of the lights didn't always work very well. It was also the most secure, with thick metal doors, heavy locks, constant video, and heavy metal tables with steel rings for cuffs or shackles. Edgar Boyle looked right at home, leaning on one elbow, his other wrist handcuffed to the table, pitch-dark eyes blazing with hot hate from beneath thick dark eyebrows. He was a large hairy man, ample tattoos displayed beneath a white muscle shirt. Short-cropped dark hair and a goatee amplified his scowl.

'Quite a record you've got here, Edgar,' Frank said absently as he stood in a corner of the room, flipping through a file. 'Juvie at twelve. Stints in a couple of prisons. Assault, battery. They know you in Reno, Bakersfield, Phoenix . . . ' He trailed off and looked at the silent man. 'Looks to me like you've never been very good at this stuff. You're a violent criminal but not a very good one.'

Boyle refused to say anything. Athena, standing in another corner, arms folded, suddenly let loose a string of what sounded like Spanish. It got a reaction. He turned to her and spat, 'Don't talk your school Spanish to me, cop. I know English just fine.'

'Just wanted to see if you knew how to speak in *any* language,' Athena said. 'And by the way, it's not school Spanish. I grew up speaking it in my home. I figured since your record says you once fled to Mexico and got extradited, you were probably fluent.'

'Reality check, Edgar,' continued Frank, 'or should I call you Mr. Black Flag? You probably thought you had stumbled onto a good thing here, with this dark web gig, but it looks as if you're not all that good at this either. We found your car. We found your laptop in it . . . and a whole string of messages. Nothing was even password-protected. You might as well have left us a trail of cookie crumbs. I'm not all that tech-savvy, but compared to you I'm Bill Gates. This is supposed to be a super-secret black-ops kind of internet, and here even I could follow the trail from your computer! We contacted the police in your home town, and there are Federal cyber-crime agents that couldn't wait to get warrants and run to your home. There are probably half a dozen law enforcement agencies crawling all over your digs as we speak.'

'You're basically screwed,' said Athena. She smiled nastily. 'I can say that in five languages if you'd like.'

'It would probably be a good idea at this point to request a lawyer,' Frank said. 'We've already read you your rights and unless you have anything else you'd like to tell us, I think we're done here.'

Edgar glowered back and forth at them and in a gruff low voice he uttered a string of the foulest, coarsest epithets Frank had heard in a long time. It actually took him aback, but when he shot a look at Athena, she was simply flashing a small tight smile. She said, 'Thanks for the input, Mr. Boyle. I guess we finally got through to you. Frank, I agree, we're done here.'

⋆   ⋆   ⋆

Garo Bedrosian was indeed surprised and delighted to hear that there were suspects in custody for the robbery of his café. When he and his daughter showed up for the line-up, Frank and Athena greeted them and explained the identification procedure. Garo Bedrosian would stand behind a one-way glass and several people would each step forward where he could look at them carefully.

'Cecilia,' asked Frank, 'you're sure you didn't see or hear anything that night?'

Cecilia shook her head. 'I came to support my dad, but really, I don't know what I can do to help you.'

'Okay, then we're going to ask you to sit out here.' He pointed to a wooden bench along the corridor wall.

'I'll stay with you,' said Athena. 'Come on.' She led her to the bench. As the two men walked down the hall, Cecilia plopped herself down on the hard bench and hung her head morosely.

'Have you spoken to your father yet about that night?' asked Athena.

Cecilia shook her head. 'I can't. I just can't.'

'You know, that day you told me about it, I can't imagine that was very easy.'

'I felt I could talk to you. You're the only woman who's talked to me. In the police, I mean.'

'Cecy, I think you felt guilty — so guilty that you needed to get something out. But I think there's still more than what you told me. I keep wondering how Tommy and his partner happened to show up right after you forgot to lock the door.'

Cecilia did not look up. 'That's what happened. Just like I told you.'

'You're, what, nineteen?'

'Twenty.'

'Okay. You're like any other normal twenty-year-old girl. You feel stuck with your father and you want to go live your own life and have excitement. So you sneak out to dance clubs with your friends, things like that. Tommy is older, and he's handsome and charming. He's got that dangerous thing going on too, doesn't he? He turned your head. I'll be honest with you: I think being charming to young women is maybe the *only* thing he's good at, but he is clearly pretty good at it. I think he talked you into helping him out, leaving the door open that night. He might have told you he needed the money to spend on you, to take you somewhere or buy you something. Or maybe he just made you feel like you wanted to be part of his dangerous life.'

'Nobody was supposed to get hurt,' whispered Cecilia, still not looking up.

'So you did tell him you'd leave the door unlocked that night?'

Cecilia froze momentarily. 'No. No, it happened just like I said. I made a mistake.'

Athena sighed and gently placed a hand on Cecilia's shoulder. 'Believe it or not, Tommy was in kind of the same position. He was trying to impress an older, more dangerous guy. But he feels like a scared, embarrassed kid right now, just like you probably do. He rolled on the older guy. Tommy's not much of a stand-up guy when you come down to it. But there's one place he is being a stand-up guy. He refuses to implicate you in any of this.'

Athena bent down to be closer to the girl and spoke softly, urgently. 'These are guys who made choices about the kind of lives they lead. You still have choices. That guilt is going to eat away at you, because you're a decent person at heart. You're going to need to take responsibility for your actions, sooner or later.'

'I didn't do anything,' Cecilia said. It came out as a sob. A tear rolled down her cheek. 'I forgot to lock the door. I forgot.' Her voice trailed off as she repeated it over and over. It was as if she was trying to drown out not just Athena but other voices within herself.

'Your father still thinks he's the one who forgot, right?'

Cecilia nodded.

Athena decided she would leave it there. It was ultimately up to Cecilia.

The two sat in glum, heavy silence, neither saying a word until Frank and Garo returned to them.

9

The morning shift would not begin for another half hour, but Frank found Athena already sitting in the cafeteria. It was really not much more than a coffee bar with a refrigerator case of day-old pastries, salads and sandwiches; but someone, sometime had seen a need to dignify it with the name 'cafeteria.' He got himself a mug of coffee and joined her at the old Formica table.

'You look downcast,' Athena said. 'How'd the meeting go with Castillo?'

'First of all, he already spoke earlier this morning with the assistant district attorney. She's declining to go after Cecilia Bedrosian. She's as overworked as the rest of us and has to pick her battles. She says there's nothing there to get a conviction.'

'That's all the prosecutor's office cares about, right?'

'Did you really want the kid to go to jail?'

'No. Cecilia's going to have to deal with her father and her own demons. I hope this has scared her and I hope she comes to terms with it.'

'Tommy and Bruno bailed on each other. She's cutting deals with them both. Bruno bragged he could do the time, and then the next thing you know, he's throwing his other partners in crime under the bus as fast as he can to try to reduce his sentence. Some hard guy. Anyway, it looks like Simpkins and Dowdy will be able to clear a couple of their own cases as well.'

'Honor among thieves.'

'Gotta love it. On the other hand, Tommy hasn't said a word about Cecilia. He's got his own weird code of chivalry, I guess.'

'Cameron Wardell has been charged too, I take it?'

'He cut a deal. So did his crackpot killer for hire, though that won't really be of much help to him. There are about four federal agencies looking into his activities as well as a few locals. He apparently negotiated assaults for hire, and possibly murders, across a few state lines. What a deranged lunatic.'

Athena stared at her coffee mug. 'Wardell's just a kid. Where does someone like him get the idea to sponsor a murder for hire?'

'Search me. I keep hearing that millennials are crazy. His deal isn't going to keep him out of a stretch in prison, you can be sure of that.'

'And what about the Bizel thing?'

'Lou tells me the Feds swooped down on the whole place last night. Sweeping indictments against everyone. Racketeering, money laundering, extortion. His contact in the Department didn't mention anything about LaRoche. I'm thinking he didn't have anything to do with any of that. He was just an opportune buyer who smelled out a bargain and didn't care that it wasn't totally legit. Lenora Park called that one right.'

'Her inflammatory story was partly responsible for motivating Wardell in the first place. I wonder how she's going to feel about that.'

'I wouldn't be surprised if it makes her

stop and think. At heart, she strikes me as a well-intentioned sort. Maybe she'll temper her reportage. It remains to be seen.'

'What's going to happen to the building, to the Del Osos?'

'Castillo seems to think that in the end Felipe will be able to get the building back. It'll be a long process, but for now he'll be able to keep the mercado there.' Frank paused. 'I guess that's about it. He asked me how you're doing and I told him you're doing fine. You did some great work your first week, you know that?'

'I don't know how great it was. To be honest, this job, this place are kind of overwhelming.'

'Your first day on the job, you went out to do a routine re-interview on a job I figured was a dead end. You cleared it. That's impressive. I would never have gotten there. Maybe I've just gotten too cynical about this stuff.'

'I lucked out. The daughter was willing to talk to me. On the other hand, I was ready to throw in the towel on Julie LaRoche. My instincts told me that had to be a random robbery, that we should pursue it that way. You knew better. You wouldn't let go and you found the key . . . and an obscure one, at that. They've always told me you're a good detective. I should have trusted you more.'

'I'm thinking we might make a good team, Pardo. You can learn from the dinosaur and maybe the dinosaur can learn from you. If you can put up with me.' Frank's smile was weary but genuine.

Athena, still staring into her mug of coffee, managed a weak smile in return. A pineapple danish pastry sat on a paper plate, untouched.

'Is it always like this?'

'What do you mean?'

'We did good this week, right?'

'We did outstanding this week.'

'So why doesn't it feel good?'

'Athena, it's not like you haven't been on the streets for a few years already. What do you expect it to feel like?'

'I know. But being in uniform is different. You see a lot of stuff that's hard to process, but there are also times when you feel you've done some good. I know it's only my first week here, but . . . aside from clearing the cases, there doesn't seem an upside yet.'

'Sometimes it feels better than others. Often, clearing the case is pretty much all you can hope for. In the end it's what we do. We try to do it well and make everyone count. It's not a warm, fuzzy job we've chosen.' He reached into his shirt pocket and pulled out a folded envelope. He opened it and handed it to her. 'Maybe this'll help.' The envelope was addressed to DETECTIVE VANDER-GROFF at the unit. 'Nobody ever gets the name right. I'm used to it.'

She unfolded the note paper inside and read the short letter.

Dear Detective Vandergroff,

I saw in the news that you had found the people who killed my father. Thank you for your hard work. I don't think many people liked my father. I don't think he exactly went out of his way to make anybody like him. He was a complicated man and I'm only now coming to grips with my own feelings about him. It would have made sense to me that nobody would have cared who killed him.

I thought he never cared about me and wanted nothing to do with me. It turns out he thought enough of me to leave me all he owned. That, and the fact that you must have gone to great trouble to find the truth behind his death, has led me to re-evaluate my father and my own family history. I think it's going to be a long process but I've taken the first step. And for that I thank you.

Sincerely,
Sarah Hartnett (LaRoche)

Athena handed the letter back. 'Well, somebody found closure. Do we ever find it here?'

'Like those new-age types like to say: it's a journey, not a destination.' Frank made a wry face. He pointed to the danish. 'So are you gonna eat that?'

She broke it in half and handed him a piece.

Frank stuffed the whole thing into his mouth and chewed it rapidly. 'Better than usual.' He rose from his seat. 'Once more unto the breach?'

'Sure. And by the way, I know that's Shakespeare.'

'And by the way, do you really speak five languages?'

She finished the last bite of her piece of danish. 'More or less. Some better than others.'

He nodded, impressed. 'Pretty good for a rookie kid. Still, maybe there's things I can teach you. Keep an open mind, okay?'

She nodded, a little grimly, and stood up, gathering her refuse and sweeping the crumbs off the table. 'I think there's a lot I can learn from you, Detective. Make no mistake about that.'

'Oh yeah, and while I think of it . . . there's something I can learn from you too.' Frank reached into his pocket and held out a brand-new smartphone. 'No more stone-age flip phone. But I'm already boggled. I think I'm going to need some help getting up to speed on this . . . and the information age in general.'

'Looking forward to it.'

Maybe this really would work out, Frank mused.